With the Heart of a Ghost

STORIES

LIM SUNWOO

TRANSLATED BY CHI-YOUNG KIM

THE UNNAMED PRESS
LOS ANGELES, CA

AN UNNAMED PRESS BOOK

Published in North America by the Unnamed Press.

www.unnamedpress.com

Unnamed Press, and the colophon, are registered trademarks of Unnamed Media LLC.

Hardcover ISBN: 978-1-961884-60-1
EBook ISBN: 978-1-961884-61-8
LCCN: 2025946375

This book is published with the support of the Literature Translation Institute of Korea (LTI Korea)

Cover artwork by Haruna Makisumi
Cover design, typeset and illustrations by Jaya Nicely

Manufactured in the United States of America by Kingery

Distributed by Publishers Group West

First edition

Contents

With the Heart of the Ghost 1

You're Not Glowing 21

Summer, Like the Color of Water 52

That Unfamiliar Night 79

Go Sleep at Home 105

The Hibernating Guy 134

Even Though It's Not Alaska 156

Curtain Call, Extra Inning, Last Pang 177

Author's Note 197

With the Heart of a Ghost

With the Heart of the Ghost

I was slumped over the bakery counter one slow afternoon. *It's so dark for the middle of the day—is it going to rain?* I wondered, looking out the window. Then I gasped at a strange sensation that felt like something was being pulled out of my body. I instantly turned as cold as a sheet of ice.

I got up from the counter and went to the storeroom. In the corner was the folded blanket I'd used the previous winter, and I flung it around myself without pausing to dust it off. It was only September, the foliage still green, but I couldn't stand feeling chilled to the bone like this. I came out of the storeroom, my shoulders hunched against the cold, and nearly fainted from fright. I stood in shock, staring at my own body. There I was, slumped on the counter, my eyes closed. So that's how unattractive my curved shoulders and my gaping mouth must look to others. I wasn't upset that I was dead. I'd just never imagined that I'd die so suddenly. I didn't have a chronic condition or symptoms of any sort; how could I die like this in the blink of an eye?

Nobody could have imagined that I'd die before my boyfriend, Jeongsu, who'd been in a coma for two years in the hospital. Would Jeongsu learn of my death? As these thoughts flashed through my head, my blanket fell to the floor, and the me at the counter opened her eyes. What the hell?! I found myself shouting. How can you open your eyes when you're dead?

Because I'm not dead, the thing answered. Not only did it look like me, but its voice was also identical to mine; the entire thing gave me the creeps.

Then who are you? I asked, and the thing answered airily, I'm you. It drifted toward me, and the closer it got the warmer I felt.

I couldn't wrap my head around what was happening. The ghost, this thing that looked just like me, explained that I hadn't died. It wasn't here to snatch my body. It didn't want anything from me. It, too, didn't know why it had appeared, but one thing was clear—it was also me.

Then tell me what you know about me, I challenged. I don't know anything about the past, it said, because I only came into being right now. I feel your emotions the exact same way you do. Happiness and sadness, that sort of thing.

So I attempted to get rid of the ghost in a variety of ways. I looked up the Lord's Prayer on my phone and recited it, I showed it a picture of an amulet, and since they say red beans chase away spirits, I ate a red bean bun. But the thing didn't budge. Seeing how unenthused it looked with each attempt at something new, I found myself hating the sight of it even though it had my very own face. Deflated, I slumped on the counter again.

I'm not an evil spirit or a ghost, it insisted. I'm just you. That's even worse, I retorted. It nodded thoughtfully and said, I know.

The bell attached to the front door tinkled. In came the old man who stopped in to buy rice-flour bread every few days. I wasn't sure how to explain that thing to him, but he didn't give it a second glance as he talked about how the skies were so overcast, paid for his bread, said goodbye, and left. Other people must not be able to see you, I commented. Maybe not, it said.

Good then, I said, perking up. You must have your own ghost life that's perfect for you, so why don't you go seek it out? I told you, I'm not a ghost, it said. Still, you can get away from me, right? I asked. The ghost pondered my question, then said, Okay, and went out through the door. The cold rushed back when the ghost moved away from me. This was a problem because I was so lacerated with cold I just couldn't bear it another moment.

I threw the door open, ran out into the middle of the street, and grabbed the ghost. My hand went straight through its body as it looked back at me. The awful cold vanished the moment I stood before the ghost. Unbelievable, I murmured. I'm just as baffled, the ghost said. Do you really feel what I'm feeling? I asked. Aren't you just describing what you can see? Anyone can tell that I'm out of sorts right now.

I was getting worked up. The ghost let me finish ranting and said, I think you're less out of sorts than disappointed.

I shut up at those words. In fact, from the moment the ghost opened its eyes, I'd been feeling deeply disappointed that I wasn't dead. In the end, we went back into the bakery together. That afternoon, I sat behind the counter while the ghost perched on it. Rain never came, even though the skies remained gray, threatening a downpour.

❁

Kim Jiwon was a regular who had been coming by the bakery every day after school for the last year and a half. She was seventeen, eight years younger than me, but we'd still become friends. Demonstrating an impressive persistence, she stopped by daily for a bun, never appearing to get sick of the routine. Another constant was that she always came alone. She never brought anyone, and she never even talked about anyone else.

This small neighborhood bakery didn't have a separate seating area except for a chair next to the ice cream freezer. That chair was Jiwon's designated seat. My favorite time of day was chatting with her as she sat there, eating some kind of bun.

On the day the ghost popped out of me, Jiwon stopped by the bakery as usual. When the ghost saw Jiwon, it got up slowly from its perch atop the counter; it moved just the way I did. Jiwon picked out a walnut bun, settled in her chair, and stared at me.

Something's off with you today, Eonni, Jiwon said. What? I said, trying to act normal. The ghost was beside Jiwon already. It had moved just a few paces away from me, but I was already so cold that I unfurled the blanket I'd rolled up in the corner and draped it over my knees. You look weird, Jiwon said. Did something happen? Nothing happened, I told her.

You really care about this girl, don't you? the ghost said to me as it looked at Jiwon. I've been feeling happy and at ease since she came in. You don't need to get involved, I snapped at the ghost, but Jiwon flinched. I panicked and explained that I wasn't talking to her. Jiwon said it was fine and gathered her things to go. Of course she would go. Jiwon thought only the two of us were in the bakery.

I felt I had nothing to lose, so I confessed that there was a ghost next to me. I told you I'm not a ghost, the ghost said, suddenly beside me again. Then how am I supposed to explain who you are? I demanded. How many times do I have to tell you that I'm you? the ghost retorted. Right now, there's a ghost standing right next to me, and it looks exactly like me, I explained to Jiwon again. And it's insisting that it's not a ghost.

A ghost? Why are you talking to yourself? Jiwon looked at me with worry. I don't know how to explain this, I said, and tried again: Earlier today, I got freezing cold, and then a ghost turned up. Jiwon studied me for a long time and said, I've always thought this about you, but you really aren't normal. Jiwon settled back in her chair, perhaps thinking I'd lost my mind or I was talking nonsense, and started nibbling on her bun again. That day, Jiwon left a little earlier than usual, and I could only hope that she wasn't trying to get away from me.

Then it was rush hour, and people flooded in. The ghost sat on the floor behind the counter. I was depleted by the end of the night, having frantically helped customers while distracted all the while by the ghost. At closing, three potato buns remained once again. We sold more than twenty kinds of baked goods, and the potato bun was the least popular. It had a crude shape and didn't taste all that good, which meant there were two or three that went unsold every day. I was the one who had to deal with the leftover buns. In the beginning, I had them for dinner each night, but they were so bland I had to find a better way to dispose of them.

Aren't you going home? asked the ghost. I told the ghost I had to stop somewhere first. It was no surprise when I discovered I had to stick close to the ghost even after work. If we were apart for even a moment, I turned so unbearably cold. We walked through the tunnel leading to Hangang River. I sat by the water, tossing potato bun pieces at the fish. I'd been doing this consistently for the three years I'd been working at the bakery. I tossed the pieces at the fish as they opened and closed their mouths above the surface of the water. Want some? I asked the ghost, but it replied that it didn't eat food.

The ghost was interested in the fish. They're such beautiful, incredible creatures, the ghost said, gazing at them. That was exactly how I felt, but I was painfully embarrassed to hear the ghost say it. I'd never uttered the thought out loud in my life. I tore the potato buns into small pieces and threw them in the water while I ate a soboro bun. The ghost stayed crouched by the water, watching them.

Do you only give them potato buns? the ghost asked out of the blue. Why? I asked, surprised. They're saying the potato buns are gross, the ghost said. The fish told you that? I asked. The ghost didn't answer as it stared at the fish. The fish frantically opened and closed their mouths, lodging their complaints with the ghost. Yeah, they're just eating it to survive, the ghost said after a moment. How would you know that? I demanded. Did you talk to the fish? Yeah, the ghost said. I felt betrayed, and instead of throwing the last piece of bun in the water, I shoved it in my mouth. I hadn't eaten potato buns in a long time, but the fish were right; it really was dry and flavorless.

Only after I ate my bun and fed the fish did we return to my eight-pyeong studio and go to bed. The ghost lay down next to me, and my small studio felt tiny. It was the first time in two years, since Jeongsu, that someone was in my bed. I wasn't sure I'd be able to fall asleep, but the ghost was so warm that I instantly dropped into oblivion.

Every Saturday I went to visit Jeongsu at the hospital. When I showed up, his parents stepped away to give us privacy. This had been happening every week for two years.

I walked into Jeongsu's hospital room, and at least for this moment I was glad to be with the ghost. Since the previous night I'd been hoping the ghost would be able to talk to

Jeongsu the way it had conversed silently with the fish. When I asked the ghost to try, it leaned toward Jeongsu and closed its eyes. After a long time, the ghost said, I don't hear anything. Can you try again? I asked. Maybe if you concentrate harder? The ghost closed its eyes again. I gnawed my nails as I watched. Still silent, the ghost reported. Okay, I said. I knew my expression was matter-of-fact, but the ghost told me not to be too sad.

I gazed at Jeongsu lying in his hospital bed. Two summers ago, he had been in a car accident in front of his house. His mother called me at the bakery. I sensed something terrible had happened to Jeongsu the moment I heard her trembling voice say, Hello? Nobody knew what he was planning to do when he left the house that day. He didn't have plans that we knew of, and he was dressed casually. I cycled through the different scenarios endlessly: Did he go out for a walk? Did he go out for a bite to eat? Was he on his way to buy cigarettes? Was he on his way to see me?

I had so many questions for him. I wanted to talk to him through my ghost. The seasons had changed eight times while I waited for answers that would never arrive. Now, I didn't feel weird talking to myself out loud, and I didn't cry in front of him anymore.

I lay down on the cot to Jeongsu's right. The ghost lay down to his left. Don't do that, you're cramping him, I said. I don't take up any space, the ghost said. I had nothing to say to that, so we ended up lying there, Jeongsu sandwiched between us. He has a Roman nose, and his eyes are so big, the ghost said, looking at him as it lay on its side. I can see why you liked him. I didn't respond. The ghost, who claimed to feel my same emotions, had just said *why you liked him*, not *why you like him*. I looked up at the ceiling as I pondered those words. I couldn't bring myself to turn over and look at Jeongsu in the face.

After a long moment, I said quietly, Hey, Jeongsu. I kept my eyes on the ceiling as I continued: You might have noticed, but I have a ghost haunting me. And so I was hoping to talk with you, but now that I think about it, you're not a ghost. You aren't a fish. You're a person. I wasn't thinking straight. I'm sorry.

The ghost sat beside me on the bus ride back home. It was weird, it said. I was lying next to him, and I felt like I couldn't breathe. And? I asked. That's all, the ghost said. I stared silently at the jet-black hair of the person sitting in front of me.

At home I washed up, turned off the lights, and lay down. I stared up at the ceiling. That was when the tears I'd held back escaped. I knew my love for Jeongsu had withered away. I'd found myself waiting for Jeongsu not because of my love for him but in order to break up with him. I cried silently for a while, still looking up at the ceiling. I knew the ghost would have caught on, but I couldn't bring myself to stop.

❊

Sunday was the one day I stayed home. I woke up and nearly had a heart attack when I saw my own face lying next to me. The ghost must have been startled, too; we stared at each other, our eyes wide with shock. It looked like I'd need more time to get used to this situation. Did you sleep, too? I asked. No, I was just lying here, the ghost said. Your mind is so busy even when you're sleeping. *Maybe it's because I was thinking about Jeongsu before falling asleep,* I thought.

A little later, I said, Make me something to eat, will you? No, the ghost said. I always wished there were two of me whenever I had to do something I didn't feel like, but now that there was another me it turned out to be no use at all.

I dragged myself up and made myself a rolled omelet. I was the only one eating, but somehow I ended up tucking away a double portion. Maybe I ate for you, too, I told the ghost. No, you just ate a lot, the ghost said. I did the dishes, worrying over how to get rid of my strange companion. Should I go to the doctor? To a church? Should I hold a shamanic rite?

A cockroach the size of my forefinger skittered along the sink. I jumped, and the ghost, who'd been lying on the floor, jumped up, too, asking, What is it? I pointed at the roach. Staring at the critter, the ghost asked me to go open the front door. I did, and the roach obediently crawled out. Stunned, I asked, How did you do that? I just asked politely for it to leave, the ghost replied. And it worked? I asked. Yeah, the ghost said. In that moment I had the nonsensical thought: *I won't need to worry about bugs as long as I'm with the ghost, so maybe it should stay until winter.*

The ghost sat by the window without a clue as to what I was thinking, watching the rain come down. It was finally raining; we'd had overcast weather for a few days. When I asked if it was bored, the ghost asked if I knew how much work it was to feel someone else's emotions. But I'm feeling peaceful right now, I said, and the ghost shook its head: From the moment I met you, you've never once been at peace.

To demonstrate how wrong the ghost was, I lay in the most relaxed position I could assume and hummed. But Jeongsu suddenly popped into my head. Jeongsu liked humming. Would he still like to hum? Would he still like alternative rock? Easy walks? Neat shirts? If Jeongsu were to wake up tomorrow, how much of him would be what I remembered? How much of him would be different?

I'd changed a lot in two years. I didn't use to like rainy days, but I now did. Instead of Hollywood flicks I now liked slow French films. My favorite kind of bun changed from sausage to soboro. But I still didn't like the potato bun I'd always hated . . .

The ghost looked at me. See? You're far from being at peace.

❋

The moment I got to work I took a folding chair out of the storeroom. The ghost had asked for it so earnestly. It's not nice to make me sit on the bare floor, it had insisted. That was why three chairs were now set up in the bakery, and how

I ended up sitting next to the ghost all day long. When there were no customers, the ghost swung its legs slowly. I'd forgotten that I used to do that. Why are you looking at me like that? asked the ghost as it swung its legs, and I told the ghost it was nothing.

I was glad to see Jiwon walk into the bakery that afternoon. I'd been secretly worried that she would avoid me after last time. She tore into a cheese roll and asked if the ghost was present. I told her it was next to me, and Jiwon asked me to prove it. How? I asked. Jiwon asked the ghost to make a roll float in the air. I told her the ghost couldn't perform tricks like that. Jiwon asked the ghost to turn off the bakery lights. I told her the ghost couldn't do that, either. It's a ghost and it can't do anything? Jiwon asked, crestfallen.

Sure it can, I said. It can talk to animals, and it feels the same emotions I feel. Then what does it say you're feeling right now? Jiwon asked. Gloomy, like always, the ghost said. It says I'm feeling very peaceful, I said. Jiwon cocked her head in disbelief and remarked that if the ghost really did look just like me, I must feel really odd when I looked at it. Does this mean you believe me? I asked. Can I be honest? Jiwon said. I half believe you and half think you've lost your mind. I told her that was fair.

I want to drop out of school, Jiwon said, finishing off her cheese roll. It's so loud at school and I'm so quiet. That made me think of Jeongsu again, Jeongsu who'd become quiet for a long time now. After Jiwon left, the ghost and I sat behind the counter, deep in thought, chins cradled in our hands as we watched dust particles floating in the air.

At the end of my shift, a single potato bun remained. I took it and a soboro bun to the river and split each in half. I would share the good and gross buns equally with the fish. As I tossed the pieces in the water, the ghost asked, How many years have you been with your boyfriend? Five years, I said. Three when he was healthy, two since he's been in the hospital.

Perhaps sensing how my mood sank like a rock, the ghost got up and went to the fish. The fish are saying thank you, the ghost said, turning to look at me. Then the ghost's expression turned incredulous. Are you *that* happy to be thanked by fish?

When did I stop hoping for a miracle? I wondered as I cleaned the store. Disappointment piled up to become rage, and rage turned into resignation. At a certain point I'd stopped wishing for anything so I wouldn't have to repeat that cycle.

This attitude of mine might have been the reason I readily accepted the ghost into my life. All week I went to work with the ghost, chatted with Jiwon and the ghost, tossed food into the river with the ghost, and slept beside the ghost. I stopped jumping at my own face when I opened my eyes in the middle of the night. It wasn't quite like looking into a mirror. The ghost had one entirely different quality despite being otherwise identical to me.

The ghost somehow reacted more faithfully to my emotions than I did. The ghost flopped on the floor when I was sad and hummed cheerfully when Jiwon came by. Once, a customer pinched the buns on display. When I said, Please don't touch the baked goods, he erupted in anger and stormed out, leaving behind all the buns he'd mauled. For the rest of the day the ghost paced the bakery, fuming. I told the ghost to stop because it was making me crazy, and it shot back, That's why you always look like you're about to cry, because you keep this all bottled up inside.

I never got used to seeing someone who looked like me acting that way, no matter how many times I saw it. I was glad nobody could see the ghost. But today, the old man came in to buy his rice-flour bread and told me I was looking upbeat. Rolling my tongue around the red ginseng candy the old man had given me, I wondered if it was because I had been thinking less about Jeongsu since the ghost showed up or because I stopped wanting to disappear—what with everything going on.

That evening, I left the bakery and walked to the river with the ghost as always. A lot of people were out in the streets, maybe because it was Friday night. The ghost and I usually walked side by side, but this time we had to go down the street single file. Tagging after the ghost, I saw for the first time what I looked like from behind. I was small, the back of my head was round, my bob didn't reach my shoulders, and I took short steps. Stand up straight, I told the ghost, who laughed, dumbfounded. The couple walking by looked at me funny.

I brought sandwich bread and a potato bun for the fish that evening. Tomorrow's the day you go to the hospital, the ghost said, sitting still. Yeah, I said. For how long? asked the ghost. My hands froze, then continued to tear the slices of sandwich bread into long strips. For a while I had asked myself that question, but had stopped at some point. Some days I thought I'd be able to wait for Jeongsu forever; a day was over once you slogged through it. But on other days I didn't think I could wait for him for another second. So not thinking about it was the best answer I'd come up with. But how long could I really keep doing this? I didn't know what to say.

The following day, the ghost lay down next to Jeongsu the instant we entered his hospital room. I cracked open the window for some air. I sat and looked into Jeongsu's face. His blank face, with his eyes closed, was now so familiar to me. I'd have to take out old photos to remember his smiling face, his frowning face, his concentrating face, his bored face.

I told him what had happened since my last visit. In no particular order, I told him the potato buns were still gross, the fish had a pickier palate than me, Jiwon was going to be a senior next year. I didn't forget to talk about the ghost. I told him living with a ghost wasn't as bad as I'd feared. I told him how the ghost shooed bugs away and translated what the fish were saying. The ghost lay there quietly, listening to me ramble.

When I was done, I took Jeongsu's hand. A cool breeze blew in from behind me, and I closed my eyes to imagine walking hand in hand with him, the way we used to every day, a long time ago. In my mind I walked with Jeongsu on the grass along Hangang River, down the streets of our favorite neighborhood, along the narrow alley in front of my place, in the crosswalk by the bakery. I wasn't sad. I wasn't scared. I wasn't heartbroken. I kept my eyes closed even after we walked that entire route. It was strange. It felt too real for it to have been only in my imagination; I was too awake for it to have been a dream. I opened my eyes. Did you do that? I asked the ghost. The ghost said it didn't know what I was talking about, but I knew it had given me a gift.

We returned home feeling happy. I washed up with warm water and had enough energy to cook myself a meal. At the sight of dishes piled in the sink after dinner, my hand lifted automatically to rest on my forehead. That gesture—I suddenly found myself on the verge of tears. Jeongsu and I had goofed around like this, placing a dismayed hand on our forehead over the most trivial of things. I would grip my forehead when my shoelaces became untied while out walking, and Jeongsu would tie them for me. He would hold his forehead if he forgot to bring the book he was going to lend me, and I would forgive him. I closed my eyes in an attempt to rein in my wobbly feelings. I felt something warm and opened my eyes to see the ghost crying.

I studied the ghost as it cried. All the emotions that couldn't fully surface in me resided entirely within the ghost. I reached out and wiped the tears flowing down the ghost's cheeks. I couldn't touch them, but they were clearly warm; they were so warm that I was able to cry. What kind of ghost cries like this? I asked. Because I'm not a ghost, the ghost said, weeping. The ghost wrapped me in a hug, and I felt perfectly understood, something I'd never before experienced in my entire life. I think this is the end, I said in the ghost's arms, and the ghost answered, Yes, it is.

❂

For a few days afterward I maintained my daily routine. I went to work and mopped the floor and sold baked goods. As Jiwon ate a custard bun, I asked her a question I'd been curious about: Aren't you sick of buns? Jiwon gave my question careful thought, then said the buns here weren't the best or the worst, which meant she could keep eating them. She said it was possible only because she didn't think about what they tasted like as she ate them.

Jiwon had so fully accepted the ghost's existence by now that she'd made up a game, trying to guess where the ghost was. She would point anywhere in the bakery, insisting she felt something damp or sensed a chilly energy, and say, There, but she was rarely correct. Even as I lived my life, joking around with Jiwon and splitting the potato buns equally with the fish, I would sit vacantly, deep in thought, in brief moments of interlude, when the bakery was empty or after the fish departed from the banks of the river. The ghost would also look preoccupied.

One Thursday evening I went to the hospital instead of the river. Jeongsu's mother was by the bed. She was surprised to see me, but she quickly looked resigned. Without asking me a thing, she patted me lightly on the back, murmuring, It's okay, I'll go get dinner. I told her to enjoy her dinner, even though I knew she was lying. I knew she sought out a deserted place, rather than the cafeteria, to sob at length.

After she left, I gazed at Jeongsu. I wanted to remember every detail. I cautiously touched his face. The ghost stayed with me the entire time, leaning against the wall. Only after a long time passed was I able to say what I hadn't been able to utter, what I had said only to the fish at the river.

The ghost and I fled before Jeongsu's mother got back. It occurred to me only later that Jeongsu's mother telling me *It's okay* might have been on behalf of her son. She might have intuited the situation in a flash, the way I had when I answered her call two years earlier. That evening, I ran away from Jeongsu, his mother, the heavy air in the hospital room, the long corridor illuminated by bluish fluorescent lights, all of it.

When Jiwon spotted me in my chair the next day, she said, Eonni, you look terrible.

I had stayed up all night. Jiwon didn't look great herself. She was coughing and sniffly. Did you catch a cold? I asked, and Jiwon answered in the affirmative. I made her a cup of hot herbal tea. Exhausted, Jiwon, the ghost, and I sat in our designated chairs and didn't speak for a while.

Jiwon broke the silence. Eonni, did you not sleep well last night? Instead of answering, I asked her, Should I quit my job? Should I quit and go live on an island down south? Jiwon asked if I was being serious. I told her I was half serious, half joking.

Eonni, you know I come here to hang out with you, Jiwon said. I don't even really like buns. You said the ghost showed up when you felt cold, so for a few days I've been sleeping with my window open. I'm so lonely that I was hoping a ghost would haunt me, too, but I didn't get a ghost, just a cold. So do you really have to leave for the island?

That day I took Jiwon to the river. At first, she was scared of the fish, but when I told her the fish were happy to meet her according to the ghost, she perked up and tossed pieces of potato bun in the water. I was wondering who ate potato buns, but I guess it was you and the fish all along, Jiwon said, looking down at the bun in her hand.

Afterward we sat by the river and chatted. I told her I wasn't serious about the island and that we could always hang out even if I quit my bakery job at some point. The ghost, who had been sitting quietly, got up. It sat next to Jiwon and wrapped an arm around her shoulders. I don't know what you just did, but it feels really nice, she said.

❁

On the first Saturday after all that happened, the first Saturday I was staying home instead of going to the hospital, I lay in bed, wondering what to do. I decided to clean the apartment for once. While I cleaned the ghost sat at the table, swinging its legs, moving them aside when I approached with the vacuum. While I was at it I tackled the pile of dirty dishes, too.

My studio was clean by the time the afternoon rolled around. I sat on the floor, feeling better as I downed the beer. At a certain point the ghost came to sit beside me. We sat there, side by side, looking out the window.

On that unremarkable afternoon, the ghost leaning against my shoulder whispered something in my ear, then gently disappeared. What it whispered before vanishing wasn't in the form of language. It was the heart of the ghost, beautiful and dreamy and feather soft, supple like fish and glistening like flowing water.

You're Not Glowing

With the rain, the roof began leaking. It started drip by drip, but then grew into a gush so strong it seemed it would punch a hole through the living room ceiling. I quickly put a pot under the leak, but it was no use. All day long Gu and I bailed water and mopped the floor, and when it finally stopped raining that evening we sprawled on the floor, spent. We turned on the TV from down there and discovered that the world was ending.

On the news, ambulances were carting away people covered in blisters that obliterated their features to such a degree that no one could tell who they were; it also seemed they couldn't move. The reporter noted that their condition was caused by jellyfish.

At night, the jellyfish glow blue along the coast. They lure people with their light, then wrap their tentacles around those who come close to turn them into jellyfish, just like them.

As the reporter said this, the screen filled with a tank containing a jellyfish and a halibut. The footage was sped up to show how, when the jellyfish's tentacles swept across the halibut, lying plastered on the bottom, the fish contorted and turned into a jellyfish. Cool, Gu said, his eyes glued to the TV. Really cool, I said. After our band split up, we had spent every second wishing for the world to end. Who knew our wish would come true so fast?

People turning into jellyfish put our leaky ceiling into perspective. None of it had really been a shock: not the band breaking up, not losing our security deposit on our rental in Seoul, not fleeing to the countryside, where we were staying in Gu's late grandmother's house with the leaky ceiling. We excitedly looked up jellyfish on YouTube and learned that people were calling them "zombie jellyfish" and that these mutant creatures had taken over not only all the waters around Korea but the world's oceans. We clicked on link after link for a while before we got hungry and made ourselves ramyeon.

❊

Two weeks had passed since the mutant jellyfish showed up. Dashing our expectations, the world didn't come to an end that easily; the jellyfish couldn't get themselves on land. Once all the beaches were closed, most people simply didn't come across jellyfish. Students kept going to school and office workers kept going to work.

Still, everyone was obsessed. Zombie jellyfish without a brain or a heart, floating in the ocean, transforming all animals they touched. They even looked elegant, staying in one place and quietly glowing, drawing people in. When scientists reported that humans might develop an urge to approach the jellyfish when exposed to their light, sales of sunglasses skyrocketed to unprecedented levels.

Everyone understood the jellyfish in their own way. Some saw the collapse of civilization. Some took them to be God, and some saw them as an exit from life. What Gu saw was an opportunity for employment.

The mutant jellyfish propagated wildly until they filled the oceans and began lapping onto beaches. The nerves in their tentacles stayed alive for a long time after death, so even as corpses they remained dangerous. They stank terribly as they decomposed. Overwhelmed by the deluge of complaints from residents living near the coasts, the government hired beach sanitation workers. Every morning, workers descended to the beaches to remove rotting jellyfish carcasses. Young men who could easily pick up and move the heavy jellyfish were preferred, and Gu soon got a gig as a beach sanitation worker.

Once Gu left for work I found myself alone at home. I submitted job applications everywhere, but not a single employer contacted me. Everyone was starting to feel the pinch since tourists were staying away from beach towns. Every day was filled with a surplus of hours, and I spent my abundant time looking up everything I could about the jellyfish. Information proliferated online, but truth comprised only a small portion of it all; one of the real facts about these zombie jellyfish was that they could see and hear—an evolution from other types of jellyfish. They were watching and listening to the effects they were having on humanity. I started to like them a little more once I learned that fact.

I would chase zombie jellyfish across the web until I looked up and realized that Gu had come home. Gu, did you know even an elephant can turn into a jellyfish in the span of a month? Looking exhausted, Gu nodded. Disappointed, I ate the nearly expired gimbap he had brought home.

It's actually a little scary, said Gu, who had been eating his gimbap quietly. What is? I asked. The jellyfish, he said. I get rid of a few hundred one day, but when I go back the next day everything is back to how it was before. And the next day and the day after that. Sometimes it feels like I'm in a weird nightmare. I wrapped an arm around his shoulders without a word. Tired Gu smelled like rotting jellyfish. Since he started this job, the stench had seeped into his body and lingered, no matter how hard he scrubbed himself in the shower.

How much worse do you think it'll have to get before the world falls apart? I asked that night in bed. I wonder about that, too, Gu said in the dark. After we moved here, we had never once talked about music. Gu had sold his guitar. I no longer hummed, let alone sang. All of a sudden, we had stopped what we had been doing every single day. It was weird.

Looking at Gu's narrow back, I played the song we used to sing together in my head. When would we be able to go back to that time? All night, rain dripped into the huge basin Gu had brought home. I fell asleep worrying. *The house won't flood while we're sleeping, will it?*

✲

There was now a new emergency number, 082, to report a person turning into a jellyfish.

Jellyfish blocked the intake of a nuclear power plant and caused blackouts in numerous places.

People wanting to live with family members who had turned clashed with the government, which insisted they be euthanized.

A video of a person weeping and hugging their dog that had turned into a jellyfish, then getting stung, racked up a million views.

A new jellyfish religion formed.

People wanting to kill themselves traded jellyfish tentacles at a markup.

Criminal organizations embraced the use of jellyfish tentacles as a new lethal weapon.

A creepy rumor went around that these jellyfish were used to make cheap gummy snacks.

Chinese restaurants pulled cold jellyfish salad off their menus.

A cosmetics brand that advertised how its products would produce jellyfish-glass skin posted an insincere apology the following day.

✲

I totally get why they came up with a jellyfish religion, I found myself saying late one night as I stuck a pain-relief patch on Gu's lower back. Gu asked me to elaborate, but I brushed it off, saying, Just because, but I was convinced by the YouTube videos I'd seen recently showing people being mesmerized by the jellyfish's glow. Maybe they were just acting, but they went straight toward the creature, violently shoving away those who tried to stop them. What struck me was their moony expressions, as though they had fallen in love.

What kind of glow did the jellyfish give off that could bewitch everyone? I envied them. I had gone on countless auditions, but nobody had looked at me like that, not even once. I still cringed whenever I remembered how a set nobody paid attention to could turn into humiliation, how songs nobody listened to could wither away.

When I finished applying the patch, Gu asked, So, did you hear back from anywhere? No, I replied. I hadn't even seen a position I would be eligible for. My coworker told me there's a company that helps people who want to turn into jellyfish, Gu said. Wouldn't you be charged with assisting suicide? I asked. It's not suicide, though, Gu explained. It's sending them into the ocean so they can live as jellyfish. He said his coworker's mother worked there and could recommend me to her company.

You go to the client's house and wait until they turn into a jellyfish, Gu said, then paused. It's run by people in that jellyfish religion you were talking about. People who believe the jellyfish are God? I asked. Yeah, Gu said. My coworker's mom doesn't believe in any of that, either. It's just to make money. I told Gu that I was in. I might never be able to make music again if I didn't start saving money. I would do anything, even if it was something worse, if that meant I could make music.

Things progressed quickly once I agreed. Gu's coworker's mom recommended me, I did an interview as a formality, and then I found myself sitting in an auditorium for training. We were to be matched with clients of the same gender.

The instructor talked about the contract the most. That piece of paper was the only thing that would protect us in case something out of the ordinary happened. As one might expect, the contract was unfavorable to the client, with a non-disclosure agreement and a clause requiring the client to accept any and all side effects that might occur during the transformation process.

After training, the company handed out bags that contained jellyfish tentacle pills, sea salt to calibrate the salinity of the water, plankton for the client once they turned, and sunglasses to protect our eyes against their glow. They were flimsy, like 3D glasses given out at movie theaters.

My first client lived in an apartment with three generations of her family. *Lee Gyeongsun, 81, is ill and wants to go to the ocean, pain-free.* This was the concise note written on the intake form. I rang the bell and Mrs. Lee's daughter opened the door. I followed her into the primary bedroom to find the low, bathtub-sized tank that our technician had installed the day before. Mrs. Lee was there, too. I said hello, and she asked me who I was. I said I was going to assist her through this process, and she asked me again who I was. I said, I'm going to help you become a jellyfish, but she kept asking me the same question. My mom isn't doing all that well right now, the daughter finally chimed in.

I understood. I asked them to excuse me for a minute and stepped outside to call my manager. I thought the client has to sign the contract, I said. How can someone with dementia give consent? She signed herself up for the program in a moment of lucidity, my manager explained. I hung up the phone and stood in the hallway for a long time before going back in to check the temperature in the tank.

What I needed to do that first day was draft the contract and help my client take her pills. The daughter signed the contract on Mrs. Lee's behalf and quickly disrobed her mother. She then helped her mother into the tank. Mrs. Lee seemed to believe it was bath time.

My mom told me she wanted to swim free in the ocean, the daughter said as she watched her mother sitting in the water, as though she knew I was suspicious of her motives. She hasn't been able to move freely for over five years, the daughter explained.

A little later, the daughter stuck the pills inside a roasted sweet potato and handed it to her mother. Mrs. Lee grabbed the sweet potato and wolfed it down without pausing to chew, and she soon began scratching at her throat and chest, screaming. Her neck swelled, red as though she had been burned.

Mom, cried her daughter, alarmed, and Mrs. Lee reached out and gripped her daughter by the arm. Is this normal? her daughter asked urgently. I reassured her by telling her it was, then injected a narcotic painkiller in Mrs. Lee's thin arm.

In the room, dark even with the lights on, we waited for Mrs. Lee's tortured groans and swearing to die down. We watched as clear blisters formed over the red marks and gradually spread over her entire body. She finally relaxed when the painkiller kicked in. When things were back under control, I explained to the daughter what would happen next.

I feigned nonchalance to reassure the daughter, but my heart was hammering in my chest. I had never seen anyone turn into a jellyfish in person. All afternoon I sat by the tank, even skipping lunch. I constantly checked on Mrs. Lee's condition, and when it was time for me to go, I gave her another shot of painkillers and something to help her sleep.

So, how was it? Gu asked when I got home. Instead of answering him, I asked him what went through his mind as he removed jellyfish from the beach. Just, Gu said, pausing his massage of my shoulders, how can I get rid of these faster? How can I make this easier?

That's it? I asked.

Yeah, Gu said. At first, I swore and spat on them, but I don't do that anymore.

That's when it gets really scary, I said, and Gu said, Is it?

Maybe at some point I won't feel anything anymore when I see someone turn into a jellyfish, I mused.

Maybe, Gu said.

You think? I asked.

Or maybe not, Gu said.

I stripped off my socks and threw them at him.

When I got there the next day, Mrs. Lee was covered in blisters. It was time for the final transformation to begin. For a human to become a jellyfish, one had to go through the process of eliminating everything. The brain had to vanish, the nerves had to vanish, and even the very last drop of blood had to vanish. When a human was stung by a jellyfish, first their features melted into one another, their upper body became a clump, then their lower body split into dozens, hundreds, of thin tentacles.

In other words, today was the last day Mrs. Lee's mind would remain intact. Tomorrow she would be a jellyfish, having forgotten everything. Everyone was home today, her daughter and son-in-law, even her two grandchildren. I waited in the living room while they said their final goodbyes, and I went back in when they emerged.

I came out after confirming that Mrs. Lee's face was gone, and the family asked me to join them for lunch. I declined twice, but they wouldn't take no for an answer. The table was laden with a feast, from galbi jjim to deodeok gui. These are my mom's favorite dishes, the daughter said. Nobody spoke a word during the meal. The kids picked at their food before heading into their rooms.

I know it might seem cruel that we didn't stop her, said the son-in-law, who hadn't uttered a single word until then, but this is us doing our best.

I understand, I said. This was the recommended answer printed in the manual, but I honestly could understand them. I knew what it was like to love something and then give it up.

When I entered the bedroom the next day, only a single jellyfish was floating in the tank. I went down my checklist and confirmed her motility and her response to food. Then I distributed sunglasses to the family and drew the curtains to darken the room. Ten minutes later, through the sunglasses, we saw a whitish glow. Mrs. Lee was finally a jellyfish. I called the technician, who arrived an hour later, put the jellyfish that had once been Mrs. Lee in a truck that had been renovated to carry live fish, and left.

As soon as I got home from work I lay down and didn't budge. People are the worst, I said, dumping my feelings onto Gu. They're completely worthless, so cowardly, and a whole bunch of nothing. Gu stroked my hair and told me my day sounded hard. My phone dinged. I took it out and saw that 350,000 won had been deposited into my account. I'm making jellyfish while you're getting rid of jellyfish, I said, and if we keep going like this, neither of us will ever be unemployed. Gu laughed. But, Gu, those people? They didn't cry. Nobody cried even though Grandma turned into a jellyfish. It's sad, I said, and Gu echoed my words back to me.

❊

Anyway, it was entirely thanks to the jellyfish that Gu and I could live like others. No longer did utility bills pile up; no longer did we need to ask friends for favors. Gu and I worked hard while unprecedented rains continued and jellyfish kept washing up on the beaches. Gu would often be called in on the weekends, too.

As for me, I was turning someone into a jellyfish every three days. There were just as many people who were tired of living but didn't want to die as there were jellyfish. As Gu predicted, I gradually became less sensitive to the transformations. Anything was easier the second time around, and the tenth time was even easier.

I could make three million won a month if I didn't take too many days off. With that amount, I had enough to put away in savings after paying for maintenance fees and living expenses. Once I saved enough I would go back to Seoul with Gu. I focused only on that whenever guilt flooded through me.

We bought ourselves certain things as we started making money. Gu bought cologne, and I got myself a lunch box. I found it awkward to eat with clients' families, and it wasn't possible to leave for lunch if a client lived alone, so I started packing my own lunch. Gu must have been self-conscious about how he smelled, seeing how that was the first bottle of cologne he ever bought. The scent was reminiscent of a green forest, far from the ocean. Gu constantly doused himself in it, but when I embraced him in the middle of the night he still smelled like salt, sand, and rotten jellyfish.

Despite the rain we took the bus to the grocery store to buy food over the weekend. We filled our basket with soy sauce and sesame seeds, green onions and a bundle of spinach, eggs. Everything felt off-kilter, because we had never cooked in Seoul. On the bus home I leaned against the window and looked out. It felt odd that we were making plans to make sigeumchi namul at home when the world was becoming stranger and stranger.

Rain had filled the basin to the brim while we were out. It feels like the rain is slimier, Gu said, sticking a finger in the basin before pulling it out. No way, I retorted. I swear, he insisted. I went to feel the water myself, and maybe it was just my mood, but it did feel slimy. Is it because of the jellyfish? I asked. I don't know, said Gu, then he went through the yard to toss it all the way outside the gates.

For dinner we had the sigeumchi namul I made alongside Gu's doenjang guk. *It's not always sad when nothing happens,* I thought as I emptied my bowl of rice. Instead of doing the dishes we turned on the TV and watched a segment about a couple who were caught raising their jellyfish child in a defunct swimming pool. The jellyfish floating in the pool was much larger than what I was used to seeing at work.

They keep growing, I realized, relieved, when Gu mumbled, Crazy assholes. Don't call people names, I said. Why not? he said. Why do you talk about people like that? I asked. Just yesterday I had sent a client, a child, to the ocean. Gu didn't answer. He stopped talking to me.

It wasn't the first time he'd given me the cold shoulder. Clips of people killing jellyfish, claiming they were paying them back for the havoc, were always trending on YouTube. The crueler the method of killing, the more views were racked up. When I told Gu, who watched them every night before falling asleep, to stop, he would put his phone down, annoyed. We would stop speaking for a short time, but the next day we would start chatting again as though nothing had happened and fall asleep together late at night, listening to water dripping into the basin.

❊

My next client was Kim Jiseon. She was fifty, worked in the service sector, and had gotten divorced three years earlier. All she had written down as the reason for transformation was: *Because I want to be a jellyfish*. I arrived at a small, old, bleak apartment building and rang the doorbell. A short, thin woman opened the door for me.

Ms. Kim said the tank didn't fit in her bedroom, so she'd had it installed in the living room. On her invitation I sat on the love seat, and she handed me a cup of coffee. She was so hospitable that it felt for a moment that I was the client. I took the contract out of my bag and showed it to her. I imagine a lot of people don't go through with it as they're filling out the paperwork, she said. I said that was correct. Her comment made me wonder if she was going to back out, but she signed the contract and swallowed the pills without hesitation. Before she entered the tank she said, I stocked the fridge with drinks. Please help yourself to whatever you want.

Clients usually started shrieking in agony within ten minutes of taking the pills, but Ms. Kim was on the quiet side. Silence filled the living room, interspersed with moans through gritted teeth. I asked her if she was all right more frequently than usual and each time got a yes.

I injected the painkillers and took my time looking around her place. The living room had only the leather love seat I had been sitting on, in addition to the tank. Clients who were single tended to get their affairs sorted beforehand. In contrast to the empty apartment, an abundance of coffee drinks and juices she had bought for me were displayed by type in the fridge. I drank an orange juice. All the while she was gradually turning transparent.

Gu called me as I made my way home. He said his coworker had turned into a jellyfish. His coworker had taken his gloves off for a second, and the remnants of a jellyfish had splattered the back of his hand. He was rushed to the hospital, and I think that was the last time I'll see him, Gu said in a low voice. Not that we were super close. He said he and their other coworkers were out to get drunk.

Late that night I went to the bus stop to walk Gu home. I propped him up the entire way. As always he smelled like jellyfish, a stench that couldn't be covered up by either cologne or alcohol. Gu, why don't you do my job? I asked, holding on to him as he stumbled along. My job isn't as dangerous. I know that's not why you're telling me that, Gu said, stopping in his tracks. You think what I do is awful. You think it's horrific that I kill and throw away jellyfish that might have been people.

I had nothing to say to that. I knew that beach sanitation workers were just doing their jobs and that they wouldn't be able to do them if they remembered the jellyfish might have been people at one point, but I found myself recoiling whenever I saw news footage of them slamming a shovel on a jellyfish or moving carcasses into a garbage truck. I couldn't dismiss the fact that my reaction had hurt Gu's feelings. I told him I was sorry, but he stalked ahead without accepting either my apology or my assistance.

The next day I sank into thought as I watched Ms. Kim turn into a jellyfish. When would Ms. Kim stop being Ms. Kim? When was the exact point in time that she went from being human to a jellyfish? The moment her face disappeared? The moment her heart vanished? Her brain? Was it stupid to search for hints of humanity in someone who had become a jellyfish?

That morning, Gu and I had acted as though nothing had happened. It did seem easier to move on, but how long could we keep doing this? I always thought about how much we had to bury our emotions, how much we looked the other way, just to keep loving each other. I checked the temperature of the water and spoke with Ms. Kim for what might be the last time. Is anything bothering you? No, came the faint reply underwater. Before I went home I added powdered sleeping aid in the tank, hoping she would sink into deep slumber, without having to think any thoughts.

When I got there the next day, Ms. Kim had finished her transformation. I was about to close the curtains to check on her glow when I heard murmuring. I put my ear close to the tank and realized I could hear a voice. Are you speaking right now, Ms. Kim? I asked, and I heard her say, Yes. Can you hear me? I asked. Yes. Can you see me? Yes.

She most certainly looked like a jellyfish, but her voice was coming out of her body. And I waited for a long time with the curtains closed, but she didn't emit a glow of any sort. Has something gone wrong? Ms. Kim asked nervously, perhaps detecting my shock. I reassured her that nothing was wrong, then stepped outside to call my manager.

Sometimes people take longer to transform, she said airily. I just haven't seen the transformation steps change like this, I explained. She looks like a jellyfish, but she still has cognitive abilities and she can talk. My manager's voice turned serious: I've never heard of anything like that. Let me check and call you back.

Back inside, I asked, Ms. Kim, are you feeling all right? I'm feeling okay, she said from inside the tank. And is the water temperature okay? She said it was, then asked, Am I glowing? I told her she wasn't glowing yet. I think we might need to wait till tomorrow, I told her.

I spent the rest of the afternoon in the quiet living room with Ms. Kim. Although she wasn't glowing, at least she had taken on the form of a jellyfish.

My manager didn't call me back until the next morning as I was on my way to work. Let's give it a week or so, she said. It's rare, but apparently sometimes it takes longer for the full transformation to take effect. We hung up without much for me to act on.

I unlocked the front door with the key I'd received the first day and walked in, and Ms. Kim asked immediately, Did something go wrong? I heard you turn into a jellyfish in three days, but as you can see I'm still the same inside. I reassured her with what my manager had told me, that sometimes it could take longer to transform. I hear it could take as long as a week, I said.

But I couldn't just sit there and do nothing. Over the next few days I attempted to turn her into a jellyfish in different ways. I gave her two more tentacle pills, turned on Bach's *St. Matthew Passion* (this had been the song in the video I'd watched during orientation), and had her follow the 4-7-8 breathing technique that was supposed to be calming.

Ms. Kim breathed in and out deeply and gradually began to move slower. Wondering if the transformation was finally continuing, I called out, Ms. Kim? and she flinched. I fell asleep, she said. You can't just fall asleep, I protested. I'm sorry, she said. That's okay, there's no need to apologize, I said.

Feeling spent, I lay down by the tank. This was how the week progressed, with Ms. Kim still able to converse and still unable to glow. She had no family we could consult about her situation. She had divorced her husband three years earlier and had cut her family off before marriage. I went to her house every day, waiting for her to complete her transformation. Today I took out the last grape juice from the fridge. I never knew it, but it turned out I preferred grape juice over orange.

❁

When the week was up, my manager told me she would be coming by. She and two other staffers arrived at lunchtime. The staffers went up to the tank to say hello to Ms. Kim, and when she responded with hello, they exchanged alarmed glances. They checked her state, which hadn't changed. After a long time, one of them said, Her transformation seems to have stalled.

My manager said there had been cases of failed transformation when the clients died before fully turning into jellyfish, but this was the first time something like this had happened. We've discussed this internally, and we've come to the conclusion that we have three options here, she told Ms. Kim. You can be released into the ocean like this, or, if you prefer, you can choose assisted suicide. I whipped my head toward Ms. Kim, but she just floated in the water the way she had been all along.

The final option was for Ms. Kim to stay in a tank in the company offices. My manager explained that though all risks were assumed by the client, the company was willing to work with Ms. Kim. Do I need to decide now? Ms. Kim asked after a pause. Not at all, my manager said. If you move into our offices, you'll have plenty of time to decide what you would ultimately like to do.

I don't want to leave my home, Ms. Kim said, which was met with silence, and, in the end, unable to stand the silence any longer, I blurted out, I can keep watch a little longer and give you a call. My manager thought about it for some time and replied that it was a plan.

I followed them out the front door and asked my manager, Would it be possible to get paid for the last week? I hadn't been paid because Ms. Kim hadn't fully turned into a jellyfish. My manager said she would authorize extra pay.

Back inside, the mood was dour. To cheer us up, I decided to replace the water in the tank with the gear my manager had left. I let out the murky water and gradually added in clean seawater. What they said must have been a shock, I said. I expected as much, Ms. Kim said, more calmly than I would've imagined. One thing that's for certain is that I won't live my entire life in a tank. I didn't think that was a good option, either, I told her.

Ms. Kim suddenly asked me if I had seen the luminescence of the jellyfish with my bare eyes. When I said no, she told me about the first time she had seen the jellyfish. She had gone to the beach the first day she heard the news about the jellyfish. I wasn't allowed on the beach, she said, but I went into a raw fish restaurant and sat on the second floor where I could look down on the ocean. The owner, who'd had to close the restaurant because of the jellyfish, had steamed some potatoes for her, and she had daubed them with salt and eaten them as she waited for the day to darken.

Back then, it wasn't common knowledge that the jellyfish's glow could entice humans, but the restaurant owner had warned her that it could make people fall into a trance. Hearing that, Ms. Kim's heart pounded. Finally, the sun set, and the ocean began glowing. Populated by hundreds, thousands of jellyfish, the ocean glowed more intensely the darker it got, as though someone had flicked on a light switch.

There was a glow, Ms. Kim told me. A brilliant, beautiful glow, something you can't find in real life. You know how, online, they make it seem like humans rush toward the jellyfish like zombies when they see that glow? It wasn't like that at all in real life. That night I just stared down at the ocean for hours. I knew I would have no regrets in life if I could glow that bright and beautiful, even just once.

Now I understood why she had kept asking me all week long if she was glowing. Why don't we wait a little longer? I asked, looking down at her floating in the clean, clear water. Instead of answering, Ms. Kim bobbed slowly throughout the tub.

The house was quiet and still when I got home. Gu hadn't worked that day, but his flip-flops were gone. He must have popped out for a bit. I put my sunglasses on and looked out at the yard, waiting for him. When I wore sunglasses in the evening, things that used to be visible were rendered invisible. Darkness concealed the clothesline and the earthenware jars lined up in the yard. When you looked at a luminous jellyfish through sunglasses, all you saw was a hazy shape, not a bright glow.

People were really fearful. Maybe the jellyfish weren't there to be God or zombies or to hasten the end of the world. Maybe they were just glowing to the best of their abilities. People, not the jellyfish, were the problem. Everyone had a fear of darkness, so maybe those who couldn't live with their own darkness were the ones drawn to the creatures' glow. I wasn't sure I would be immune to the glow, though. I had never taken off my sunglasses to gaze upon jellyfish.

I sat on our small porch and looked into the darkness until Gu came home. I greeted him, still in my sunglasses. He said he'd gone on a nighttime walk. I feel like you haven't taken a single day off lately, he said, settling down next to me. Yeah, a client's taking a long time to transform, I said. You must be exhausted, he said, and held my hand. Then he said, I was thinking about opening an installment savings account.

Gu, are you happy these days? I asked, looking at him. Instead of answering me, he replied that here, he wasn't scared about the future. I fixed the ceiling today, he said. Now it won't leak when it rains. I leaned my head on his shoulder and thought, *His shoulder feels muscular*, then realized I wasn't at all thrilled by the fact that the ceiling was repaired. My heart actually sank at the thought that we might be staying in this house for a long time. I was glad he couldn't see my eyes behind my sunglasses. *What I know for sure, Gu,* I thought, *is that I haven't really left Seoul or music. I've just drifted all the way here.* I was still scared about the future. But

I told him I was glad he'd fixed the ceiling, that it was a great idea to start saving. I told him I was happy he was doing well. I did mean that last sentence.

❁

At work, they said we had to maintain distance from the clients, but that wasn't always successful. It was even more impossible when you spent so much time with the same client. A week passed after my manager stopped by, and with the second change of water I started calling her Jiseon instead of Ms. Kim.

Recently I had begun worrying about her; she was shrinking, even though I was giving her plankton for meals every day. It appeared that a jellyfish, which should be in the vast ocean (suddenly I wondered if my first client, Mrs. Lee Gyeongsun, was doing well out there), struggled to thrive when kept in a small tank for a long time. In the last two weeks Jiseon had stopped moving or talking as much.

It's not looking good, is it? Jiseon asked me one day, and I couldn't answer right away. My manager had told me to help our client come to terms with her situation, but for the past week I had kept repeating to Jiseon that we should wait and see, wanting to make her desperate wish to glow come true. But I couldn't bring myself to say that again today.

I've been thinking, Jiseon said. I think I must have held out subconsciously so I wouldn't turn into a jellyfish. You see, I'm very good at holding out. I stayed in my marriage for over twenty years, and I do things to the bitter end. I thought about what she was saying and said, If you've been holding out to stay human, there must be a reason for it. That made Jiseon think. After a long time, she blurted out, Could it be? She hesitated, then told me there was someone she wanted to see. There's someone I've liked since last year, she confessed. I've been wanting to see him before I turned into a jellyfish and even after.

My manager called me on my way home that day. She had been calling like clockwork for the past few days, and every day I asked for a little more time. At the end of the same conversation that day, she said, It just ends up harder for you if you keep digging your heels in. She wasn't wrong.

I told Gu I didn't think I would be able to pay my half of our living expenses this month. The extra pay I got from the company had been ridiculously low. That's okay, I can cover it, Gu said. Are you still with that client? Yeah, there's a problem with her transformation. What are they going to do? he asked. They said we can send her into the ocean or help her die, I told him. That makes sense, he said. It's not as easy as it sounds, I said. Then what, are you going to take care of her for the rest of your life? You haven't been paid for two weeks. Gu paused, then continued. If you're going to keep living like this, then what did we give up music for? With that, he went out.

I thought he'd gone out for a smoke, but he didn't come back until late at night. He couldn't have gone to the beach, but he reeked of jellyfish when he lay down next to me. That night in particular the smell made my insides churn, and I lay there quietly, holding my nauseated stomach. I couldn't believe that he had given up music. I never had. When had he given it up? I had always been hoping to return to our previous lives. Since when had he begun thinking of a new future? Since when had we become these people, spending all day together without sharing anything that mattered?

The next morning, instead of going to Jiseon's apartment, I went to the juk restaurant in her neighborhood. The restaurant was tiny, with only three tables. I had vegetable juk for breakfast, and when there was a lull between customers, I went up to the counter and asked the owner if he knew Kim Jiseon.

He didn't recognize her by name, but when I told him she used to come every evening for a bowl of juk, he instantly knew whom I was talking about. I haven't seen her in a few weeks. Is everything okay? he asked. Well, see, she's become a jellyfish, I answered, as nonchalantly as possible, but the owner was so shocked that he was rendered speechless. I quickly added that she was still herself. She's at home, I said. She's at home as a jellyfish? Yes, she looks like a jellyfish, but she's still herself, I said. The owner didn't seem to fully comprehend what I was saying, but I plowed on. She would like to see you. Me? Yes. Why? The owner seemed taken aback at the sudden invitation. I hesitated for a moment before answering, Because this is the end for her. The owner mulled it over and accepted. We had dinner together here, just once. She was a nice person—I'm sad to hear this.

That afternoon I told Jiseon that the juk shop owner would be coming by on Wednesday. Oh, because the restaurant closes on Wednesdays, Jiseon replied. Wednesday was two days away. Jiseon and I had decided to see this to the end. If she couldn't glow because of her feelings for him, she would have to face him to rid herself of the regret.

Plus I was getting increasingly impatient. Jiseon had become so small by now that the tank looked vast in comparison. Are you in pain anywhere? I asked, and she answered that she was just feeling weak. I leaned against the warm, heated tank. Did you try the juk? she asked. Yes, it was really good. After some time, she asked, What did you think about him? He seemed nice, I said. He's a little oblivious, Jiseon said, then added, I'm glad he's like that.

After work I paced the neighborhood for a long time and went home to find Gu already asleep. Earlier that morning, Gu had apologized about the night before instead of brushing past it like always. It still didn't feel the same between us, because we were still in this predicament of no longer understanding each other. Gu still couldn't understand why I kept going to Jiseon's, and I couldn't understand why he wanted to continue living this life.

I lay next to him as he slept and tried to remember the moment I fell for him. I thought and thought, but I couldn't remember. I remembered so many other moments. Gu tuning his guitar, Gu watching with amazement as rain dripped into the basin, Gu scratching the back of his neck when he was nervous. The Gu in my memories sparkled, brightly.

When did Jiseon fall for the juk shop owner? The very moment she pushed open the door to the restaurant? At that one single dinner they had together? I thought I could understand. Hot juk that would not have cooled, down to the last spoonful, in the round bowl. The juk shop owner had a similar warmth to him, and Jiseon would have noted that warmth, that glow. And yet the reason she was forced to give up hope was evident in the wedding band on his finger.

❁

On Wednesday morning, the bell rang at Jiseon's apartment. The juk shop owner's left shoulder was wet; it must be pouring. I led him into the living room and gave him a cup of warm tea. I offered him the love seat, but he politely declined and sat on the floor by the tank.

I brought your favorite juk, but I don't know if you would be able to have any, he said to Jiseon. I appreciate the gesture, she said. I've been wanting to thank you for a while. Because—here Jiseon paused for a moment—your juk is so delicious. Will you be able to turn back into a human again? asked the owner. Probably not, she said. We can just chat. What should we talk about? he asked. Do you remember eating together at the restaurant? she asked. Of course, he said.

I left so they could talk privately. I returned after a long walk in the neighborhood and found them laughing. I have to get going, he said as he got up. If you're still here, I'll be back to see you. Thank you, Jiseon said, but I'm going to be released into the ocean next week. The owner stood by the tank for a short prayer before he left. He added that he hoped she would be free and safe in the ocean.

After he left, I asked Jiseon if she was really thinking about being released into the ocean. No, she said. Then you should have told him to come back next week, I said, but she said this was all she wanted. Then she added shyly, Don't you think he'll think about me whenever he sees the ocean? I told her he most certainly would.

In her empty apartment I drew the curtains, and we waited for her to glow. In my head I sang all the songs on our first album, but she still didn't glow. You're not glowing, I said. No, she said.

I wasn't expecting her to glow. When the juk shop owner stepped inside and the air in the apartment shifted, I realized I had been thinking about this all wrong. Upon laying her eyes on him, Jiseon had chosen to keep loving him instead of giving up. Loving someone was so human, and the way she was shy and then sly and then laughing made it clear to me that she was more herself now than she had been at any other time. I suspected she would forever stay herself rather than turn fully into a jellyfish. At the same time it occurred to me that I couldn't do this job anymore.

Do you think it'll stop raining tomorrow? Jiseon asked, cutting through the silence. Only the sound of the rain rapping at the windows filled the stillness. Yes, it'll be clear tomorrow,

I said. I didn't know what tomorrow would bring, but I wanted to tell her something nice, whatever it may be.

The next morning, the rain had thankfully stopped when I opened my eyes. It's nice today, Jiseon said when I got to her apartment, and I told her it really was. She asked if I could take her out of the water. Her tone of voice was the same as when she was talking about the weather, so I nearly told her I would. Stunned, I asked, What's this about, all of a sudden? Is it because of yesterday? No, she said. I just don't want my final moments to be in the tank. I know my end is near.

I was contractually forbidden from any physical contact with the client, and pulling her out of the water would clearly amount to murder. But . . . I said, looking down at Jiseon, who was limp at the bottom of the tank. After a long time, I said, If you change your mind you have to tell me right away. I will, she said. She asked me to put her in a sunny spot. I put on protective gloves and carefully lifted her out of the water. I moved her to a cushion placed on the wood floor.

Light filtered through the huge living room window, reaching Jiseon. It feels nice and warm, she said. I could see her beginning to disintegrate in the sun. With a dry rag I wiped the water pooling around the cushion before suddenly realizing she was crying.

I feel drowsy . . .

. . . like I'm going to fall asleep, she said.

Instead of telling each other thank you and sorry, we sat for a long time in the sunlight together, and that was enough. Time passed and the sun was setting. It was starting to get dark. Jiseon broke the silence, her voice filled with awe. I'm glowing!

I looked over, but she looked the same as always. Jiseon, I called, uttering the name I had called more than a hundred times over the past three weeks. For the first time there was no answer. I closed my eyes and said my final goodbyes to her. I wiped the water around the cushion and emptied the tank. Afterward I sat on the love seat. Jiseon must have always sat on the right side, because the leather on that spot was more supple.

I sat there for a while, then called my manager. Ms. Kim Jiseon passed away today, I said. I thought she would ask me what exactly happened, but she just said a technician was on the way. I asked where Jiseon would end up, and my manager told me her body would be released into the ocean, just like living jellyfish. I was glad. She was going to end up in the ocean after all. Before I hung up I told my manager I was quitting. She didn't ask for specifics. Almost immediately after hanging up, three million won was sent to my bank account.

I stared at the zeros, not sure if it was severance or hush money, then looked up. The time Jiseon had spent holding out seemed to have pooled in this apartment like water in the tank, and I started thinking about a lifetime of holding out, of merely enduring. My feelings turned deep and dark, so I closed my eyes again and thought about the glow Jiseon claimed to have seen. Where had that glow come from? Was it as brilliant and beautiful as the glow she had seen long ago on that beach?

I picked up my phone and called Gu. Gu, I said. Yeah, he responded, and I didn't say anything else. Right before he was about to hang up, I called his name again. Gu, I'm going to start singing again. I'm going back to Seoul today. This time, Gu was silent. I gripped my phone tight. After a long time, he said, Go ahead. With that, our call ended.

I looked at the empty tank and thought about what lay ahead of me. I would leave Gu tonight and take the overnight bus. I would sing again and fail again, or maybe I wouldn't. But while the bus took me farther away from the shore, I would think about what Jiseon had seen, about her light that had glowed just once.

Summer, Like the Color of Water

It happened the day I brought home those gloomy mangoes. I was waiting for the light at the crosswalk to turn green on my way home from work, but it was taking forever to change. That's when I glanced at the fruit truck beside me and saw mangoes rather than the more common apples or pears or jujubes.

I didn't really like apples because they looked useless, and I didn't care for jujubes because they looked disgusting. But these mangoes somehow appeared to be deep in thought, somewhat melancholy. Maybe it had to do with what they were thinking about. I immediately liked these mangoes. I selected two that appeared the most proper, and when I got home I opened the door to find a strange man in my apartment.

☼

I wasn't one to never expect an intruder in my studio apartment. After what I went through when I was eighteen, I believed anything could happen in life. I was about to slam the front door shut and call the police from the hallway when the man called, Help me! I glanced back at him despite myself. He was facing the other way, his expression concealed from me.

Who are you? I asked, and the man asked me, Isn't this Seonyeong's place? Seonyeong . . . ? A beat later, I said, Ah. This man had to be Seonyeong's boyfriend. She was the previous tenant. When I came to check out the studio, I'd decided on the spot to take it, and asked the broker when I'd be able to move in. Hearing that I would have to wait at least two weeks, I asked, Two whole weeks? Hearing this rhetorical question of mine, it was Seonyeong, not the broker, who asked me if I had a place to stay in the meantime. When I told her I didn't, she offered to let me stay with her until she moved out.

I was anxious about living with a perfect stranger, and in a studio at that, but I shouldn't have worried. Seonyeong was so busy with work that she was never home. So I was able to use the space as if it were mine alone. We did spend a couple of lazy weekend afternoons and a few nights together, and during one of those times she told me that her live-in boyfriend was currently away for his mandatory military service. It had been an offhand remark, and I'd forgotten it.

Are you Seonyeong's boyfriend? I asked the intruder. He said he was but didn't turn to face me. She moved out a month ago, at the end of her lease, I explained. That makes sense, he said. I thought things didn't look right, even if Seonyeong's tastes had completely changed. That comment worsened my already bad mood, and I asked him to please leave. Believe me, I really want to, he said hesitantly, but I can't seem to move.

That's not funny, please leave, I said, with a smile at first. I'm really tired right now. I tried getting angry and grabbed him impatiently by the wrist, but his wrist was shockingly hard, like a plaster cast, like I was touching the cold shell of a turtle—a feeling entirely distinct from the solidity of bone and muscle. I kept feeling his wrist, bewildered, until he asked very politely to please stop touching him.

Can you check on one thing? he asked. What do my feet look like?

I glanced down to a horrific sight. Long, thick, bizarre cords had burst from his feet to grip the floor. Let me call 119, I said, deleting the 112 I had punched in my cell phone for the police and pressing 119 instead for emergency services. Your feet seem . . . bolted to the floor. Wait a second, he said, I think I know what happened to me. Which is what? I asked. I think I've turned into a tree, he said, looking at me. I looked back at him. We stared at each other.

A week ago, in the barracks, I got a letter from her that she was breaking up with me, he said, slicing through the silence that stretched between us. So you came to the apartment even though you're not together anymore? I asked. This was my home, he said, we split the security deposit fifty-fifty. I let him continue. I wanted to see Seonyeong one last time, so I thought, *I won't leave until she comes back, I'll just lay down roots here, and then I really did lay down roots*. But this is *my* place now, I said. Well, he said, that's why I want to take it back, but it's not working.

I looked back down at his feet. On closer examination they did appear to be tree roots. How about I dig you out? I asked, gently nudging the thinnest root with a finger. Ow! he shouted. Don't touch it! I'm sure it'll hurt only for a second, I told him. Don't you think you're being a little too callous because this didn't happen to you? he said. If you don't want me to call 119, we should at least repot you at your own place, I reasoned. This was when he told me he didn't have a place of his own. He had been discharged from the military the day before, but he couldn't afford rent with only half the security deposit at his disposal. So now what? I asked, frustrated. Could you call Seonyeong for me? he suggested. I think I could move if I see her.

I'd been planning to eat my gloomy mangoes then go to bed, but here I was, calling Seonyeong for the fifth time in a row. She didn't pick up. Maybe she'd deleted my number. When I hung up again without managing to speak to anyone, the intruder said anxiously, I have an idea. Could I stay here just until we get hold of Seonyeong? Of course you can't, I said. Please, he said. I'm facing the window, so I can't see what's happening behind me anyway. We can't live in a studio apartment together, I snapped, and picked up my cell phone from where I'd tossed it on my bed. I really was going to call

119 this time. But he started pleading: Please. Please help me. He was crying, which made me a little uncomfortable. I tried to wipe his tears with a tissue, but they were sticky like pine sap; I had to use a warm, wet towel to clean his face. Unfortunately, I had a soft spot for sad people.

What had happened to me when I was eighteen was the death of the only person I'd loved on this Earth. Sujin. Sujin didn't talk much, but when she did she spoke only beautiful words. Beautiful words that made me sad when I ruminated over them later. I loved her delicacy and how precarious she seemed and her low voice; I loved her more than myself.

That was two years ago. It felt like a very long time ago, but when I closed my eyes it was as if it had happened just yesterday. I didn't want to find myself in a situation where I had to care for someone, but, again, anything could happen in life. I thought about Sujin as I looked at this man who had turned into a tree. I thought about sadness continuing, accumulating. No, that wasn't true—I actually didn't think about anything.

Isn't it hard to just stand there? I asked. He said he was okay, that he wasn't hungry and didn't need to use the bathroom. He was just parched. I brought a cup of water to his mouth. Water dribbled out even when I poured it slowly in his mouth. I don't think this is how it works, he said. Then how does it work? I asked.

Following his instructions, I gently watered his feet. There we go, he said, closing his eyes with relief. I wasn't thrilled but decided to let him stay for a short bit, remembering how Seonyeong had let me stay with her for two weeks.

That night I had unsettling dreams. I dreamt that I kept inviting stranger after stranger into my home. Then I woke up in the morning to see a stranger, the tree, standing in my studio. I tried to determine which was worse, my dream or my reality, then gave up. I called Seonyeong again. She didn't pick up. I had to change in my damp bathroom, which made my new T-shirt wilt. I opened the curtains before leaving. Bright light pooled at his feet. I'm off to work, I said. Have a good day, he said.

❁

I worked at a small independent movie theater located in the basement of an old, decrepit commercial building. We had one fifty-nine-seat theater. We'd never had a fully sold-out showing. Even fewer people came by after COVID, so we now had three screenings a day, down from five. While those three films played, I sat at the small table that was the ticket booth and the concession stand and the information desk. The basement theater was dark and chilly year-round, but I liked the sound of the film playing on the other side of the thick doors, the dust floating in the air, and the smell of cheap air freshener.

And the silver metal benches. When I sat at my table, I looked directly at the benches placed side by side. People waited for their movie on those benches, reminding me of pigeons roosting on a perch. They sat in a single row, their shoulders hunched against the chill of the basement, or they dozed, or they murmured quietly. Then, when their movie was about to start, they flocked into the theater. A little later, a new group would cluster on the perch.

It might be obvious by now, but there wasn't much for me to do at work. So I thought about a lot of other things in addition to thinking that people were like pigeons. About the man who'd become a tree in my studio, about the mushrooms growing in the theater's storeroom, whether two kernels of corn could pop into the same exact shape, and about Sujin.

Sujin.

Sujin.

Thinking about Sujin didn't make me sad or heartbroken. Thinking about her was as natural as the pigeons flying in and out of the theater on schedule. At the beginning, I couldn't stand it when I thought of something to tell her as I ate or as I put my shoes on. Whenever that happened, I lifted my phone to my ear. People would think I was calling a lover, a friend, an enemy.

My phone rang. It was Seonyeong. What's going on? she asked. I missed so many calls from you. I told her that her ex was at my studio. He says he can't move until he sees you, I reported. Then he won't move, she said. No, I mean, I said after a beat, he's turned into a tree.

But I can't come, she said. I'm at a temple right now. A temple? I asked. Yeah, I'm in training, she said. After we hung up, she texted me.

If he really turned into a tree, just chop him down.

I wondered what kind of training she was in.

When I got home, he was still standing there, at attention. We exchanged awkward greetings, then I put two convenience store dosirak in the fridge and heated one in the microwave. He declined my offer of a dosirak, saying he hadn't felt even the faintest pang of hunger since turning into a tree.

I got hold of Seonyeong, I said as my dosirak circled in the microwave. Did she say she's coming? he asked. No, she's at a temple and can't leave, I told him. Do you mean she's a monk now? he asked. I don't think so, I said, thinking about her text. Did you tell her I turned into a tree? he asked. Yes, I said. And she still won't come? he asked. No, I said.

My dinner was ready. I unfolded a small table and sat down by him to eat. She's cold like that, he said, no blood or tears in her. Did you know she let you stay so she wouldn't need to pay rent for two weeks? When he said that, I realized I'd paid rent those two weeks. *No wonder she went out of her way to be nice to me,* I thought as I chewed.

When I didn't react, he said cautiously that he would try to move if I could give him a few more days. He claimed he pondered all day over how he could get himself to move. Did you find a solution? I asked. I think I'll be able to move if I stop thinking about her, he said. That's it? I asked. Yes, he said sheepishly.

I kept eating, and when I was done, I remembered the mangoes I'd bought. I took a mango out of its black plastic bag. What's that? he asked, catching sight of it out of the corner of his eye. A mango, I told him.

He seemed interested, so I stood while slicing the mango, so he could see. This mango looked gloomier than the day before, having ripened further, and the pit revealed itself when I cut it in half. But the pit was much too large, like something was wrong, and I understood why the mango had looked so morose. It had no choice but to be sad with this bizarre pit inside.

Anyway, the mango was very sweet, and I thought it would be nice if this entire space could be filled with gloomy mangoes. I would have to plant the pit as a first step but didn't feel like bothering right then, so I just left it in the sink.

He said he was thirsty, so I brought him a glass of water. As I slowly poured the water by his feet, we told each other our names. His name was San.

As I ate the mango I told San that I would give him a week. I'm calling 119 at the end of one week, I warned. A week is plenty, San said, sounding much more relaxed. You turned into a tree over someone you'd get over in a week? I asked. No, I mean she'll come by then, he said. I told you she's at a temple, I reminded him. I know Seonyeong; she'll call tomorrow, he said.

I studied San, who kept parroting the same thing. Did his brain harden as his body hardened? But when I lay in bed I remembered that plants feel pain, too.

In the middle of the night I felt something tickling my arm, startling me awake. San was standing ramrod straight by my head. I thought you were a ghost, I said. San said that wasn't entirely wrong. I was wondering if I'm really alive, he confessed. Can you sleep like that? I asked. I don't sleep but do something similar, San explained.

I lay quietly in bed, having given up on sleep. Aren't you bored just standing there? I asked. It's all right, San said. I'm good at waiting. By the way, what do you do for a living? I work at a movie theater, I said. What do you do there? he asked. Something similar to what you're doing, I said.

Did you know the sun gets so strong in the afternoon that it can make you dizzy? San asked. You should have said something, I said. I'll draw the curtains before I go to work. No, don't do that, he said. I like waiting for the light to change because it feels like I'm doing something.

My fingers crept along my itchy arm until I found a mosquito bite. I told San there was a mosquito in the room and he said he knew. Right now it's sitting on my calf, he said. I got up stealthily and turned on the light. There really was a mosquito on his left calf. I slapped the mosquito, but it flew to San's right thigh. I swatted it again. Did I get it? I asked. No, he said.

Still, he said, getting slapped makes me feel more awake. Yeah? I said, perking up. Can you move, then? No, he said.

Since I was already up, I opened the curtains. The faint light reflected off the privacy wall outside and brightened the room. I lay there until it was time to go to work, bathing in the light with San, scratching my mosquito bite. I ate the remaining mango for breakfast, and before leaving, I took out my old cell phone and turned on the radio for San. I didn't forget to water him.

❁

When we screened a long movie, I sometimes snuck out for a short walk. A narrow, peaceful canal was a ten-minute walk away. The canal was shallow and thin, freezing frequently in the winter and drying up when there was no rain. But summer was a season of abundant water, and for at least three months, water flowed, twinkling and sparkling.

I leaned over to look down at the water and sometimes listened to music, using the MP3 player Sujin gave to me as a gift. When it broke last year I'd brought it to Yongsan Electronics Market to get it fixed. The shop owner took it apart as he told me the building we were in was slated to be demolished.

Today I looked at the shimmering water. Even though I didn't want to think about anything other than how I liked the color of water, I ended up murmuring, Sujin, I'm sorry, but this isn't my kind of song. And, Sujin, now I know that sorrow makes people act in ridiculous ways. Back then, I hadn't understood why Sujin lopped off her hair with kitchen shears, why she'd walked around aimlessly for five hours at a time, why she'd given me her MP3 player, her most treasured possession.

On my way back to the theater I stopped by a convenience store and bought myself ice cream. In front of the store, two school-age kids were sitting at a table under blue striped umbrellas, staring at something intently. I approached and saw a caterpillar pooping on the table. The insect pooped, then crawled for a bit, then pooped, and the cycle continued. The poop on the table looked like Morse code. Maybe the caterpillar was trying to communicate through its poop. Unfortunately, I didn't know how to read Morse code; I asked the kids, but they didn't know, either. Perhaps sensing its efforts were futile, the caterpillar stopped pooping, and we quickly lost interest. We parted ways without saying goodbye.

Every time I sneaked back into work, I imagined something bad could have happened in my absence. Like someone having stolen cash from the counter, or the theater in a state of chaos, or the owner waiting for me, though he showed up only once in a blue moon. But, as always, nothing of note had happened, and I sat down with a pang of disappointment. I was sweating even though I'd just stepped out for a moment. I wiped my forehead with the back of my hand and texted Seonyeong, telling her I hadn't managed to chop San down so please come see him.

Who is it? called San when I opened the door. You know, this is *my* place, I said. And Seonyeong? he asked. She's not here, I had to tell him. The radio DJ erupted into laughter right then, and I had to rush over to turn off the radio.

Wasn't it too loud? I asked. Way too loud, he said, I regretted it in the first hour. Even so, he told me everything he'd heard on the radio. I ate my convenience store dosirak while being subjected to stories about strangers the entire time. This one person's hobby is to sit on the stairs of their building and drink, San informed me. And this other person goes around with a whole pepper in their bag, and another person was proposed to in the bathroom. This person, that other person . . .

I gathered that people wanted to talk about themselves. I still didn't know what that felt like. When Sujin died I didn't want to talk to anyone. I'd lain in bed with the blankets pulled over my head, though it was the middle of summer. A snowstorm raged in my heart until it froze and covered everything up. Some weather patterns changed only after many seasons.

Are you listening? San asked. I stared at San without a word. Why do you always eat convenience store dosirak? he asked. Because it's easy and it tastes good, I said. San started telling me about some other person who'd gotten hooked on cooking every day. While he went on, I was bitten again, this time on my thigh, and I failed yet again to kill the mosquito.

I washed up with cold water and came out of the bathroom, and San asked if I could turn off the AC. He said he had been waiting to ask because he thought I must be hot. I realized that San was standing right in front of the AC, where the cold air hit him with full force. You don't have to be so polite, I said as I dried my hair in the fan's breeze. I didn't think you'd let me stay, San said. *Tell me about it,* I thought. None of what I'd done felt like my choice: leaving home as soon as I turned eighteen, working at a movie theater in a basement, visiting the canal, keeping a human tree in my home. Sometimes it felt like my anxiety was living my life for me. I combed my hair back and said, Don't be too grateful, because I *will* dig you out in six days.

But a little later I changed my mind and thought San *should* be polite and grateful. Without AC, the studio felt like a steam room. I went to change the fan speed from medium to high and accidentally nudged one of San's roots. I apologized and looked at it closely. Was it just me? It looked bigger than yesterday. Root, growing, growth point, I murmured to myself, then remembered the mango pits in the sink. I went out with a container and dug up some dirt from the flower bed in front of the building. Back inside, I planted the mango pits, and San encouraged them, saying, Grow big and strong.

Were San's roots growing, too? I worried as I lay in bed in the dark. What was going to happen? Maybe San's roots would grow deep and take over the basement, maybe even climb the walls and take the entire building. *I'd probably be able to live here for free if San became the building itself,* I thought as I fell asleep.

When I woke up I smelled something unfamiliar. I wondered where I'd smelled it before, because I had at some point. It smells like san, I blurted out. Am I stinky? San asked. No, not you, I clarified. It smells like the real san, the mountains. I sniffed the container planted with the mango pits. That smelled like dirt, different from the scent that was wafting gently throughout the room. Are you sure it's not me? San asked. I went closer to sniff him and realized he was the one smelling so fresh and green.

You smell like real trees and dirt, I was going to say to him, but then noticed that sticky tears had tracked down his face; maybe he had cried overnight. I brought a wet towel and wiped his face. Aren't you going to work? San asked, embarrassed. It's my day off, I told him. I get a day off a week.

I opened the curtains, and we looked out. We were on the first floor, so you couldn't see anything other than the white privacy wall directly across the way. They claimed it was for our privacy, but people kept illegally dumping trash or peeing on our side of the wall, invading our privacy. Seonyeong had complained to the landlord, who then hung a mirror on the wall, a round mirror with a red label calling it the Mirror of Conscience. There's no way that's going to do anything, Seonyeong had snapped. In truth, the mirror hadn't done much to help.

Had San heard about the mirror from Seonyeong? I wondered, but didn't ask. There was still no response from her. I wondered what I should do, then sent her another text.

You left a pair of jeans here.

By the way, San said suddenly, I'm going to send my story in to the radio. You can win an electric rice cooker. If I win you can cook at home! I knew I wouldn't cook just because I happened to have a rice cooker, but I told him that sounded great. What story are you going to send in? I asked. How I turned into a tree, San said with a serious expression, so I just told him okay. We decided that San would dictate his story to me, and I would upload it to the radio station's website. San talked earnestly about how he'd turned into a tree. How he was dumped and roots sprang from his feet. How he subsisted through photosynthesis instead of eating. How, at night, instead of dreaming, his thoughts flowed by very slowly. There were parts I hadn't known about. At the end he said he wouldn't go looking for Seonyeong even if he could move. A moment later, he said, No, actually, please delete that. A few more moments later, he said, No, actually, please put that back in.

I was so tired after writing it all down that I made myself an iced coffee. I poured some out for San and some on the mangoes I planted yesterday. The pleasing coffee scent filled the room as the three of us enjoyed our drinks.

I hope she hears my story on the radio, San said. Do you think they'd listen to the radio in the temple? I asked. Wouldn't they listen to the Buddhist channel? he suggested. Do they tell love stories on those channels? I asked. We thought it through and decided to send San's story off to an afternoon program helmed by a singer he liked. Apparently if your story was selected, the DJ played a song that went with your story.

That evening, for the very first time, I got something for free at my go-to convenience store. A new item—a crabmeat croquette. It's expired, but it's only thirty minutes past expiration, said the clerk, who had an eyebrow piercing. It's on the house, you're a regular here. I said I appreciated it but no thank you, telling the clerk, I'm allergic to crab. But you've had crab fried rice before, the clerk said. That's okay because it's just imitation crabmeat, I explained. This has to be the same thing, the clerk insisted. There's no way they'd use real crabmeat for something we sell in a convenience store.

But it *was* real crabmeat. I'd taken a bite of the croquette on my way home, trusting the clerk's logic, but my throat began to tickle the moment I swallowed. A rash bloomed around my mouth. I rushed home.

Did you get beat up? San asked, concerned. No, no, I said, rummaging through my medicines to find an antihistamine. I'll get them back when I can move, San vowed. Just pay the rent, why don't you? I said. Your voice—you sound like a goat! San exclaimed. Please stop talking, I said.

I threw everything I bought in the fridge, took the antihistamine, and lay down. The fan's cool air gradually deflated my swollen face.

Seonyeong came up with great nicknames, San mused. She used to call me Cucumber, before we were together. Why? I asked. She didn't really like me, but I turned up wherever she went, he explained. At the department offices at school, at the extracurricular clubs, at the bars, like cucumbers that are always added to her favorite jjajangmyeon or gimbap. But she took it back when we became friends.

Personally, I'd never heard such a sad nickname. Seonyeong had called me North Korean Spy, because I listened only to

Sujin's MP3 player and didn't know any of the new songs Seonyeong listened to. What are you, a North Korean spy? she'd ask over and over. I liked that nickname. I liked imagining that there was another world I belonged to, somewhere that wasn't here. I'd even vowed to try living like a spy.

The problem was that I didn't have any useful information I could hand over to someone. All I knew was this: that a person could live off convenience store food, that water glistened in the narrow canal every summer, that you occasionally got an answer as you talked into a phone that had dialed no one. Who would want this kind of information? It didn't seem like anyone would, so I gave up trying to be a spy, and Seonyeong moved out before she could give me another nickname.

As I was about to fall asleep, San said quietly, Maybe Seonyeong isn't going to come. I wanted to tell him something reassuring but drifted off. The next morning, my rash was gone without a trace.

❁

During the showing of *Farewell My Concubine*, the second film of the day, I was standing by the bloated canal; it had rained overnight. I wondered what kind of expression Leslie Cheung was making right now, then realized that as of today San had been in my studio for a week.

Time had blurred while I ate convenience store dosirak, watered San and the mango pits, and wiped San's face when it occasionally became sticky. Every time he cried he gave off a fresh green scent. What did crying have to do with the smell of freshness? I wondered. I had no idea.

Water rushed in the swollen canal. Listening to the roar of the water, I kept thinking about San. Seonyeong hadn't reached out even as the week passed by. His story hadn't been chosen by the radio station, either. San listened to the program daily, hoping against hope. He talked more and more to himself. Why didn't it get picked? he'd ask himself, then say, It's fine. What good will it do to have her hear it?

Now that I was thinking about her, I tried Seonyeong again. A voice informed me that this number was not in service. I kept the phone to my ear. Sujin, what should I do? Sujin didn't answer me.

I couldn't decide what to say to San even as the third and last film ended. I opened my front door, having failed to come to a decision, and San skipped his usual greeting, saying excitedly that he had something funny to tell me. A little while ago, this guy peed on the wall, he reported. I told him that wasn't funny at all. But he peed while looking into the Mirror of Conscience! San said. I burst out laughing, even though I couldn't tell exactly what was so funny about it. San laughed, too, and as we laughed together I realized I couldn't bring myself to tell him to leave today. I decided to tell him a little later.

I have a friend who hums when she pees, I said. Whenever we went to the bathroom together I'd hear her humming, and eventually I could only pee if I heard her hum. Surprised, San asked, You went to the bathroom with your friend? You know how people go to the bathroom together when you're in school, I explained. I had no idea, San said. I didn't have a lot of friends. I remembered that San's nickname used to be Cucumber and felt a little bad for him.

Does San know it's been a week? I wondered, but I learned the answer in the middle of the night. A long time after I turned off the lights, San told me quietly, Thank you.

❊

The heat wave had begun in earnest. The fruit truck by the crosswalk began selling summer fruit like chamoe, and at the theater we were showing animated movies as a vacation special. The kids coming to the theater were more like flying squirrels than pigeons. Perhaps thrilled to be out and about after a long period of being sequestered at home, they ran around the small lobby, wearing their face masks. I had to catch each one and take their temperature before letting them in.

Today I gave San two cups of water. We compromised and turned on the AC in little bursts at a time. We had been living together for more than ten days now. I had heard him thank me in the middle of the night, so it felt awkward kicking him out now; I was also worried about him, having noticed that he was talking less than usual these days.

On the eighth day, San started spending long stretches of time quietly, with his eyes closed. He still listened to that radio program he liked but spent the rest of the time in silence. Watching him as he stood there with his eyes closed, I got worried that he'd keep his mouth sealed and turn into a real tree. He didn't even get bitten by the mosquito. He was fine, even while I was bitten regularly.

My bites itched again when I thought about the mosquito. I scratched my arm and my calf and the back of my hand. Strangely that mosquito bit me every other day on a single body part before disappearing. A very deliberate mosquito with extreme self-control. Once, I kept the light on late into the night, waiting for three hours for it to appear, but it never did. It seemed to have decided to sip my blood all summer long. At this rate I might end up a pile of skin and bones by the end of summer. If Seonyeong decided to come back, she would find only a tree and a heap of leather, two parched and wilted mango trees, and a single calculating mosquito.

On my way home from the theater, I purposely walked around the back of the apartment building. It had occurred to me that I'd never seen San from the outside. When I did, I realized he was so prominent that I was amazed there hadn't been any complaints about him. I tapped lightly on the window, and San's eyes flew open in surprise. I slid the window open. What are you doing there? San asked. Nothing, I said.

I stood in front of the privacy wall and watched San, then tried picking up the Mirror of Conscience next to me. It was much heavier than it looked. I wrenched it up and brought it to the window. I stood in front of San and slowly turned it so he could see the graffiti on the outer wall of the building, the streetlights, the nameless weeds. San looked intently at the reflected scenery. I wanted to show him the street around the corner of the building, but I couldn't capture it no matter what angle I moved the mirror in. That's okay, San said, I've seen plenty.

San said he had something to show me, too. What is it? I asked. Come closer and look, he said. Mango sprouts had emerged in the container on the sill.

As I ate ice cream before bed, San mentioned that the story we'd sent in had played on the radio. You're telling me this now? I asked. It was so short, he said. I searched the radio show on my phone and played it. It's after this part, said San. We cranked up the volume and held our breath. *Next is 0623's story. He turned into a tree after a breakup. He's standing in one place all day long, waiting for her to contact him. To 0623, experiencing your first-ever breakup, here's a song to help you keep going.* That's it? I asked. Yes, San said.

We listened to the song without speaking. *Goodbye, cold nights, goodbye, cold nights.* The repeating verse made me think that *cold nights* sounded like *coal nights*. In my mind, San, now a tree, was burning black into small lumps of coal.

But this isn't my first-ever breakup, said the small lump of coal. I dated this girl for a week in high school. I had a crush on her for a year, and when we actually started going out, my feelings for her changed. So I avoided her for a while. It's like you're being punished for that, I said. No, San said, I got punished right away. Not too long after that I logged in to this game I liked to play, and my avatar was standing in the market, buck naked. No cool hat, no pointy shoes, no cloak. She'd hacked into my account and sold everything I owned for pennies. Ever since I turned into a tree, I've been thinking about my avatar. Isn't that weird? I didn't think that was weird at all; in fact, I wanted to be friends with his high school ex.

Other short snippets flowed by after San's. We kept listening to stories that weren't all that sad or all that interesting. At some point a fresh green smell filled the room, but when I looked over at San I noticed that he wasn't crying. *He can smell like the mountains even when he isn't crying,* I realized. That scent brought me back to the canal and how I knew time was passing even without having to look at the water flowing by. Now, both San and I could miss someone without feeling sad.

❁

I imagined that I might die in this position and be discovered a corpse, my head buried in my arms on the table that stood in for the ticket office and concession stand and information desk. An unfortunate moviegoer would mistake me to be asleep when I was really dead and sit patiently on the metal bench waiting for me to wake up, until finally, when the movie was about to start, approaching and shaking me. He would push my hair back, thinking it odd that I wasn't moving, and let out a sharp scream. I would be loaded into an ambulance, which would drive off quietly without any sirens since I was already dead, and I would begin popping up in that poor moviegoer's nightmares.

The theater would finally draw widespread attention. People would say it was a haunted indie movie theater. Then again, even if I did die and haunt the theater, that wouldn't be enough to get people to flock to the place. Even before COVID, indie theaters were vanishing left and right, and it didn't surprise anybody when this type of business shuttered. If anything, they found it strange we were still open.

I was still alive and well, so it was more likely the theater would vanish before me. Then where would I go? If the theater folded, I would get a job with plenty of sunlight and fresh air. I could take my security deposit and buy a food truck and hawk corn dogs. I could load San in the food truck, and he could stand still and travel the whole country. I brought up that idea as I watered San and the mango sprouts that evening, but he declined. He said he got carsick.

Nobody walked into the theater the next morning. Maybe it was my fault for imagining it going bankrupt. Never before had it been this dead. Then I learned that there had been an outbreak at the hospital nearby. So I decided I'd be the one to watch the movie. It was the theatrical release of *Pat & Mat.*

In the movie, Pat and Mat burned down the house while trying to grill and the chicken was sucked into a ventilation fan. They were sitting in rocking chairs and were also sucked out through a window. I laughed each time. These were situations that would bring anyone to tears in real life, but it made me giggle, like Pat, who was happy the meat was grilled even though the house had burned down, and like Mat, who made a hammock out of the broken bed. I stayed in my seat for a long time after the credits rolled. Thankfully a handful of people came in for the second film.

I got home and stood stock-still by the entrance for a while, unable to move. The room was vaster than usual. I slowly took my shoes off and went to San's spot. *He did it,* I thought. I looked down at the torn, dented floor and thought back to the movie I saw earlier today. I found myself on the verge of giggles. I spotted a note beside the mango sprouts. I read it, then watered the sprouts. Just because San was gone didn't mean I could turn on the AC whenever I wanted to. The mango sprouts were still here in my studio, this species that grew in tropical climes.

I stood in San's spot. I could see only the faded wallpaper and the privacy wall outside the window. I couldn't believe San had managed to watch only this one bland scene the whole time. I stood tall and tried not to budge, until it turned dark and the streetlights came on. When the darkness grew heavier, I moved as though released from a magic spell, went outside, and stole the Mirror of Conscience.

I leaned the stolen mirror against the wall by the foot of my bed. When I lay down to sleep, it looked like another woman was lying there, her feet against mine. I propped myself up in the darkness and gazed at her. I lay down, and it felt like she was gazing at me. Now that things were like this, I prayed that if the mosquito was here tonight it would bite her, not me. She tossed and turned for a long time, making it hard for me to fall asleep, but once I did I dreamt of mangoes hanging heavy in a tree filling the space. When I woke up I felt lighter than ever. I didn't have any new mosquito bites, either.

The doorbell rang in the afternoon, and I opened the door to find a box on my doorstep. It was the gift from the radio station. Inside was a pair of terrifying acupressure slippers. Initially I didn't know why they'd send acupressure slippers to someone nursing a broken heart, but understood the instant I put them on. My feet were in so much pain that I felt extremely awake. I practically crawled to the fridge, took out ice cream, and opened the curtains. Outside stood a girl in a school uniform.

She was smoking a cigarette in front of the privacy wall. She said something when our eyes met, but I couldn't hear her through the closed window. I opened the window. What happened to the guy who used to be there? she asked. He said I could smoke here. I told her to go ahead and smoke. That guy can move now? she asked. He said he'd turned into a tree. I was shocked that someone else knew San as a tree. He'd never mentioned this girl.

I don't think he's a tree anymore, I said. That sucks, the girl said. He was cool. Yeah, he was, I said. So is he coming back? she asked. Yeah, I said, and I wasn't lying. In San's note, he'd written that he'd be back to fix the floor. But why are you so stiff? she asked. Are *you* a tree now? No, I'm wearing acupressure slippers, I said. She nodded and took another drag. Her face was bare, maskless, and she sucked the cigarette exactly the way someone I used to know would. I couldn't tear my eyes away. I ate my ice cream, watching her. For a split second, it felt like time was sparkling, flowing like the color of water.

Where did that mirror go? asked the girl after she finished her cigarette, looking around. I stole it, I said, and took off my slippers to bring the mirror to the window. You're pretty weird, too, she said, as she smoothed her long hair, staring into the mirror. When she was done, she said, See you later.

That Unfamiliar Night

When I saw Geumok again, it was in front of exit 4 at Sinchon station. I didn't recognize her right away. I merely thought, *She looks familiar . . .*, and nothing more.

The first thing I noticed was her huge cross. I had come up the escalator to find a cross standing still amid a current of people rushing by on the sidewalk. I stared at it and ended up locking eyes with the woman below. She was wearing the giant cross on her back and shouting loudly at people walking by. Be born again with a new spirit! That was when I remembered her. Geumok. I hurried past as quickly as I could, but then I heard, Is that you, Huiae?

Geumok, whom I hadn't seen in twenty years, was very small. She was tiny when we were in junior high, and it seemed she hadn't grown an inch since.

She grabbed me by the wrist. It *is* you. It's really you, Huiae. My Father must have listened to my prayers. For a split second I thought of Geumok's father, but then figured she must not be referring to him.

I can't believe I bumped into you here, I said. I've been in Seoul for a few years now, Geumok replied, then said without pausing to take another breath, You know, Huiae, I was saved by my heavenly Father. You remember those dogs? I helped them get saved, even the tiny newborns. Her hand trembled as she spoke, and I found myself pulling my wrist out of her grasp. Sorry, Geumok, I'm late, I said. It sounded like an excuse even to me. She took something out of her back pocket and pressed it into my palm. It's my business card, she said. Call me.

*

Blue towel, then white towel. White towel, then blue towel. I was sitting on the couch, folding towels. Before we got married, back when we were just living together, I had asked my husband for one thing and one thing only. Let's use separate towels. He was extremely hurt. But I couldn't blithely brush away the germaphobia I'd developed during my long years of dorm living.

I began drying myself with his towel last year, without prompting, after we realized we were infertile. We had used birth control for the first two years of our marriage and had been trying for a baby for the last two, but it wasn't working. People said you got pregnant when you were ready. Two years ago we stretched our budget to buy a three-bedroom apartment. We had sex like clockwork, timed to when I was ovulating. No baby, though. As time ticked on, I tried to show the universe how ready we were by taking on increasingly trivial things.

My father-in-law suggested around that time that we consult a doctor. They say it gets harder when you hit thirty-five, but you're already pushing forty, he said. *So's your son,* I replied in my head. But now I had no choice but to go to the doctor he recommended.

Once my father-in-law learned that we had been trying for two years, it became harder and harder to decline his kindness, though it certainly didn't feel like a kindness. I took mystery medicinal herbs he procured for me and responded to texts that pinged at all hours about how he had his fingers crossed for happy news. I ruminated about it all until I noticed that I was folding the towels sloppily. I unfolded and refolded them. This time, Geumok popped into my head. I wouldn't have bumped into her if I hadn't been going to the doctor my father-in-law had recommended.

I found her business card in my bag. Inside a sky-blue circle was a picture of Jesus, his arms open wide. Jesus inside a circle—this was the cult that had been on the news a few times. The card was printed with the same slogan Geumok had been shouting in front of the station. *Be born again with a new spirit.*

The bottom right corner had a blank white box in which she had written her name and phone number. I had never seen a business card like this. It felt alien, and I found myself slowly rubbing the name *Choi Geumok* with a finger.

A truck was what came to mind when I thought of Geumok. When I was younger that truck had ballooned larger and larger in my mind until it later became as large as a house, and only after I was grown did I acknowledge to myself that the size of the truck had been a trick of my imagination so that I would feel less guilty.

It was during the last drawing contest of junior high. Everyone had scattered around the reservoir near the school, and a few were headed to the empty lot to smoke when they discovered the dilapidated truck. They checked it out and determined that everyone had to see it, so they called everyone over, loudly.

Its front wheels were stuck in the mud by the road. Once a crowd had gathered, one kid picked up a stick and used it to move aside the tarp hanging over the cargo hold. Only then did I understand why they had been so amped up. Inside the truck were dogs, sixty tiny puppies that had died in the heat. A terrible stench assaulted our noses; they had already started to decompose.

Things unfolded quickly from there. We learned that the truck was owned by Geumok's father, a dog breeder, and Geumok became persona non grata to everyone. I was Geumok's best friend, but I was also included in "everyone."

Once, I watched a video of how an ice cream bar is made. In the machine, the stick was inserted into liquid, frozen, spun, and wrapped. Geumok's fall from grace proceeded just as smoothly. Fifteen-year-old Geumok went through the process of being whispered about, cursed, and excluded, step by excruciating step. The video ended when the ice cream was sealed in a pretty wrapper, and just like that, my memories of Geumok were hermetically sealed in junior high.

Feeling out of sorts, I picked up my phone. I texted two junior high school friends I had stopped talking to two years ago. *I met Geumok today. Remember her?* Seconds before I hit send, I changed *met* to *bumped into.*

☼

I started using a different exit after I bumped into Geumok. It added five minutes to my walk, but that was preferable. I couldn't bring myself to see her wearing that cross again. That first day, my old friends texted back like molasses. *Who's Geumok again?* said one. *OMG in Seoul?* the other said; she knew even less than I did.

I decided to cast her out of my mind. I was distracted anyway, because we were trying artificial insemination for the first time. I had to inject myself every other day. I had to get a sonogram during my period. I didn't have any room for Geumok in my life. For a whole day it felt like I had a stitch in my right side. I told my husband, and he thought it was a positive sign. I felt my belly, and it was a little bloated. I was two days late, too.

On the morning of my blood test I woke up an hour earlier than usual. My husband was about to get ready for work. He held my hand for a quick prayer. I told him to focus on work. After he left, I washed my face for a long time with cold water. Even so, the moment I stepped outside I couldn't catch my breath; the heat was oppressive. Last week hadn't been this hot.

It was worse on the subway. I ended up in a car with weaker AC. There were too many people; I couldn't move to another car. I kept bumping into the people next to me, so I wrapped my arms around my belly. *I'm being ridiculous,* I thought, but didn't lower my arms.

8.5. I stared at the *8* and the *5* written on the test strip. They said the number had to be more than 100 for a pregnancy to be possible. I told my doctor that my period was late and that my side ached. The doctor said it was probably from superovulation. I left the clinic and took a few steps when I felt a dull pain in my lower belly. It couldn't be. I headed to the bathroom on the first floor of the medical building. My underwear was streaked with blood. I hadn't even brought a pad, in case I jinxed myself. I went back up to the doctor's office for a pad.

On the verge of tears, I went back into a bathroom stall. But I couldn't cry. Instead I had to squat on the floor of the stall for a long time because of the pain. The pain didn't go away; my calves ended up numb. I finally got up and headed to the closest subway entrance. I spotted Geumok from far away but couldn't turn back. The heat and the pain made my vision cloud over.

Huiae, you look like you're going to faint. Geumok's voice sounded far away, even though she was standing right before me. I felt her holding me by the shoulders and studying me. I think you need to go to the doctor right away, she said. I told her I had just seen the doctor. It's just cramps, I said. I got my period. Then Geumok said something to someone beside her and helped me along the sidewalk.

Where are we going? I asked. Geumok said she lived nearby and that I should lie down for a short while. We went down an alley, climbed a small hill, and stopped in front of a tiny corner store. She put her key in a green metal gate next to the store that opened to reveal stone steps. We went down the steps and opened another door. That was where she lived.

Geumok's place was less a house than a room, less a room than a storeroom. It was just a single room with a sink in it. She unfolded her mat and blankets for me as soon as we stepped inside. I lay down, and it smelled like fabric softener. The room was so tiny that I could see everything she was doing.

First she put the cross down. A loop was secured to the top of the cross, and when she hung it on a nail the cross filled the entire wall. I feel like I'm an offering or something. I had meant to think that, but it ended up tumbling out of my mouth. Geumok laughed out loud. I guess you're not feeling that awful, Huiae.

Geumok said it would be good for me to eat something warm and brothy. I told her I was fine, but she said she had to eat, too. She washed her hands and began peeling potatoes. I watched her quietly. As she peeled potatoes and sliced young zucchini and chopped onions, she seemed to become an entirely different person from the one I had just seen on the street. *She's just like how she was in junior high,* I thought, then dozed off.

When I opened my eyes, she had laid out a whole spread. You should have woken me up, I said. You woke up at the perfect time, she said, placing her spoon down. She asked how I was feeling, and I told her I felt a lot better.

Steam was curling up from the freshly made gochujang jjigae. I tried a spoonful. It was shockingly delicious. The potatoes in the jjigae were soft and warm. There was also roasted seaweed and stir-fried julienned potatoes, and I kept reaching for the potatoes, seasoned simply with salt. All of this is so good, Geumok, I told her again and again. I ended up emptying two bowls of rice. After the dishes were cleared away, we sat across the small, low table. She handed me something warm to drink. I took it, thinking it was coffee, but it was sungnyung.

Geumok told me she had come to Seoul five years ago, after burying her father. She initially stayed in one inn after another, but then got a job as an assistant at a Sinwol-dong beauty salon. The owner paid her a very low wage but let her sleep in the supply closet. Geumok said she had once spent up to ten days in the beauty salon without stepping foot outside. She felt so nauseated from the chemicals that she lost eight kilos. That was when she'd met Suhui. Suhui was the only one in the salon who could cut short styles, and she was also the only one who called Geumok by name.

That was the sole reason Geumok was drawn to her, and they soon grew very close.

What happened after that was as I had suspected. One weekend, Geumok went to a gathering with Suhui and was surrounded by people who smiled like Suhui, spoke like Suhui, and called each other by name kindly. It was such a typical initiation into a cult that I found myself glad nothing terrible had happened to her.

For a really long time, Geumok started again after a pause, I wondered where things had gone wrong. That was when I realized it was because I had committed a grave sin. Huiae, when you start believing, things that used to be hard aren't hard anymore. She gazed at me quietly. I chugged down the cooled sungnyung so I could get out of there.

The days of sex becoming homework and a period indicating failure continued. At the doctor's office they referred to sex as homework. You should do your homework on this date, the doctor would say without even a hint of a smile. After the first failed round of artificial insemination, I, too, stopped smiling at that expression. We went straight into the second round. I made my husband promise not to tell his father.

I became touchier as I was injected with more hormones. The day before, I discovered a spot on the water glass I was about to use and almost threw it at the wall. I kept dreaming that I was sitting smack-dab in the center of an empty classroom. I trembled with fear that I would die the moment someone stepped inside the classroom. I had this same dream every time I was stressed. So I nearly shrieked as I walked out after a sonogram, when someone grabbed me by the shoulders from behind.

I was so startled that the girl who had grabbed me kept apologizing. I said it was fine and asked who she was. You're Geumok's friend, right? she asked. She looked like a college student. She said she was doing missionary work with Geumok and had seen us exchanging greetings from time to time. After eating a meal with Geumok, I had gone back to using the exit she was stationed at.

The girl said she wanted to chat with me. Should we grab coffee nearby? she asked. I didn't answer, instead casting around to find Geumok. I saw the cross looming above the crowd a distance away. I told the girl I would talk it over with Geumok first. Geumok saw us and ran over.

The girl suggested to Geumok that we all go sit somewhere cool and talk. It's too hot out here, she explained. I made an uneasy face. Geumok glanced at me and said we had plans today. The girl asked if she could come along, but Geumok said, Next time.

Thanks, I told Geumok. We had walked away to avoid the girl and were now heading toward her place. Why don't we grab a bite since we're already here? I'll make you kimchi jeon, Geumok said, and I didn't refuse. After all, we couldn't go to a restaurant with her cross. I asked to use the bathroom once we got to her place, but I looked around and didn't see one.

She told me it was on the second floor of the building and handed me a roll of toilet paper.

It's not an ideal place to call home, Geumok said when I returned. It's really a storeroom for the corner store. But it's my own place, my first studio in Seoul. She said that she lived in the youth lodging facilities after she was born again and that she had found herself a place of her own, here, for the very first time in her life.

Geumok told me to sit away from the portable stove, since the oil would splatter. I watched as she fried jeon on the low table.

Is there something in Sinchon that brings you here so often? she asked. My in-laws are near here, I said, and she turned to look at me. Oh, silly me. I didn't think you'd be married. I told her I'd been married for four years. You must have looked beautiful in your wedding dress, she said. I quickly told her I didn't know how to get in touch with her to invite her to the wedding. She nodded. I only got a cell phone when I came to Seoul, she said. I never needed one before.

She had fried up three kimchi jeon in the blink of an eye. How did she make them so crispy? Her jeon were crispy all around. She let me in on a secret, that you had to add just a little oil to the batter. We had Sprite with the kimchi jeon. They went surprisingly well together. I told her it was delicious, and she murmured, I know you're just being nice. When you really like something, you clap with your spoon and chopsticks.

What was she talking about? Then I remembered. She was talking about my habit from back in junior high. Oh, I stopped doing that in high school, in the dorms, I said. We had a really scary dorm teacher. Geumok said she'd liked the sound I'd made, clapping my spoon and chopsticks together. It makes the food taste even better when you hear that, she said.

As I started in on the second kimchi jeon, I asked Geumok what the youth lodgings were like. Really tight, she said. Eight of us slept in a room this size. It was so cramped that we had to keep our shoes stacked one on top of the other. Geumok placed one hand over the other to show me. I was having a hard time imagining a space smaller than this. But I liked sleeping there, she said. You'd sleep holding hands with the girls sleeping next to you. We held hands and prayed together. Then everything felt less scary.

After leaving the youth lodging facility, Geumok told me, she couldn't sleep for a month. Her hands had felt adrift. So she developed the habit of sleeping with her hands clasped together. Still, it gets a little lonely here, she said. Will you come and share a bite with me when you have time? I pondered her question for a moment, then told her I would.

When I got home that night, I gently held my sleeping husband's hand. I held it until my palm got sweaty. Still, my anxiety didn't go away. Words like *forever* and *eternal* swam around my head. I rubbed my belly that had been shot up with ovulation-inducing medication. As I was about to slip my hand out, I felt my husband tighten his grip. Maybe I did understand what Geumok was talking about.

From then on, I had a meal with Geumok every time I went to the doctor. Usually it was once a week, but sometimes it was two or three times a week. We never made plans to meet. Geumok was always there when I came out of the doctor's office; I would go up to her and say hi, then wait for her in the nearby McDonald's with a cheap cup of coffee. Then Geumok would come find me about half an hour later.

I learned why I always bumped into Geumok. She proselytized in front of exit 4 at Sinchon station from nine in the morning to six in the evening, Monday through Saturday. She was there all day, other than to break for lunch, which they took in shifts. As I began frequenting Geumok's, we settled into a natural routine. She would cook, and I would do the dishes. I could bring groceries if there was something specific I wanted her to make, but nothing could cost more than ten thousand won. Ten thousand? I asked, and she said firmly that anything beyond that was too much.

I set certain strict rules, too. Don't proselytize to me, I said. But . . . Geumok trailed off. Otherwise I'm going to feel too uncomfortable to come over, I said, and Geumok replied earnestly, I won't, I swear. Not that she never talked about religion. I know that my Father has sent you to me, Geumok said as she sliced scallions for stir-fried squid. I would have died if I weren't saved, Geumok said as she rehydrated seaweed. We wouldn't even need laws if everyone believed, Geumok said as she seasoned bean sprouts.

Each time I changed the subject swiftly. Can you add red pepper powder in the bean sprouts? I would say. Then Geumok would stop and look for red pepper powder. It wasn't too bad if the God talk stayed at this level. Most crucially, in this five-pyeong room, for a brief moment, I could be free from baby fever. All I did was watch expectantly as a dish was completed and eat it with gusto. That was all that could happen in that room.

When the second round didn't work, I was able to accept the results more readily than the first time. Maybe it was because I now had a relief valve. Everyone else around me turned intense. The doctor began actively recommending IVF, and my husband became noticeably anxious. He even skipped dinner the day we heard the second round hadn't worked. Then he parked himself in front of the computer all weekend to look for new doctors.

We argued, too. Because I said I didn't want to do IVF. But we should try everything we possibly can before giving up, he insisted. But I'm the one getting the procedure, I said. I get to choose whether to do it or not. He went outside for a cigarette. He had quit smoking two years ago.

The next day, I bought tteok and cheongyang chili pepper after my appointment. I want really spicy tteokbokki today, I told Geumok. She said she had also been craving something spicy. We agreed to add five peppers to the sauce.

I had to throw open the window while the sauce cooked down, unable to handle the spice any longer. My nose was running. It's because we're getting older, Geumok said, placing the tteokbokki pot on the table. Now, when I eat something spicy, I end up having to wipe my nose the whole time, she said. With each bite of tteokbokki we had to take a sip of water. We ate like that for a while, then Geumok suddenly sprang up. She grabbed a bottle of soju from the fridge. The bottle was already half empty.

Let's just have one glass each, she said. We downed the water in our cups and poured soju. I felt buzzed despite barely wetting my lips; it had been a while since I'd had a drink. I told Geumok that I was going through a rough patch with my in-laws and might not be able to come by for a while. Geumok said she was also going to be busy because she was in last place this month. Last place for what? I asked. Just last place, she said. We're both a mess, huh? I asked. Looks like it, she said. Cheers, I said. Before we do, Huiae, come by sometime, even if you don't make up with your in-laws, okay? Geumok said. Okay, I told her. Then let's cheers for real, Geumok said. Okay, I said.

❋

I felt a cool breeze when I opened the window. Fall had arrived earlier than expected. The season of Chuseok. My head pounded just thinking about going over to my father-in-law's. I had to go over the day before Chuseok to start cooking, and early on the morning of I would have to prepare food for the ancestral rites. Ever since I got married, I had done this every year without fail.

I went out to the living room and found that my husband had set out breakfast for me, along with a note. *Hope the appointment goes well today. I'm sorry.* A sliced omelet made with minced carrots and ham was arranged in a pretty rectangle. Still on my feet, I cut a piece and put it in my mouth. The carrots were hard, not cooked all the way through. *Thanks for the omelet, it's great,* I texted my husband, and put the rest in the fridge. I couldn't eat anymore because of my nerves.

Today was the first day on our IVF journey. A few days ago, I had watched a TV show featuring a comedian who was in front of the camera for the first time in three years since having a baby. She was giving a tour of her place. She was interviewed at her kitchen table, and I noticed the foam protectors on each corner of the table. Bright yellow pieces of round foam were glued to the wood table. I stared at them until the interview ended. And I thought, *I can handle a little more intervention if it's to make a life filled with things like that.*

On my way out of the doctor's office I found myself yearning for Geumok's place. I had heard a litany of instructions and possible side effects, as though something bad could happen the very next day. So I gave an uncharacteristically huge wave with both hands when I spotted Geumok standing in front of the station. You were acting like a little monkey, Geumok said with amusement as we walked toward her place. I laughed. Is there something you want to eat? she asked. Anything, I told her. I have eomuk at home, she said. Great, I said. Okay, she said.

But her braised eomuk tasted funny. She tried a bite and frowned. I must have added vinegar instead of cooking wine, she said. I told her it was fine, but she insisted on ordering two bowls of jjajangmyeon. The food arrived almost instantaneously. Eomuk would taste amazing with jjajangmyeon, I said. I mixed the jjajang sauce into the noodles, then tried some with a piece of eomuk on it instead of pickled radish. It didn't taste amazing.

Geumok barely touched her food. Aren't you going to eat? I asked, and Geumok put an eomuk in her mouth but quickly spat it out. It's inedible, she said as she put it in the sink. That's okay, even monkeys fall out of trees sometimes, I reassured her. That's not it, she said. She gripped the sink and stood still for a moment. I looked up from my bowl.

I think I'm going to be moving far away, she said. Last week, after service, the lead missionary had pulled her aside and suggested that she wrap things up within the month and move to a farm owned by the group. You see, I haven't converted anyone in months, she said. He told me I would be given a chance to be born again as a new worker, through farming.

The problem is, Geumok said, then paused, there's nothing there. They say even the cell service is spotty. There are still places like that these days? I asked. Right? she said. She sat back across from me. Should I go? I hedged at her sudden question and said, I don't know, but she waited stubbornly for my answer. If you want to, wouldn't it be good to go? I finally managed.

Geumok told me not to do the dishes today. She said it was only fair that I don't do the dishes since the eomuk came out bad. I glanced at her face, then said okay. She had turned quiet after bringing up the move. She said she was going to skip her afternoon shift. All I could do for her on a day like this was to leave early. I told her I could see myself out.

As I placed the jjajangmyeon bowls by the green metal gate, I discovered a small black doodle. I looked at it more closely and realized it was a drawing of a snail. *I'll show Geumok next time,* I thought. She would definitely like it; whenever she sent me a note in class, it had always been something meaningless. Once, I unfolded a note from her to find a drawing of just a single acorn, which made me burst into laughter. *I'm sure it'll be fine,* I thought as I walked down the hill. *I'm sure she'll figure it out.*

⁂

It's looking good, the doctor said, looking at the sonogram. Three follicles were growing on the right and five on the left. I followed the doctor's finger to stare at those eight black circles. I would have to wait until they grew to be at least two centimeters in diameter. I made an appointment for two days later, got my prescriptions, and walked toward the subway station.

I slowed down as I approached exit 4. In front was a hunched woman selling chewing gum. I went over to check her face. It wasn't Geumok. I hadn't seen Geumok last time or the time before then. Once I even waited for her at McDonald's for more than two hours. I wondered if she'd gone to that farm she'd mentioned, so I asked the girl who'd been out there with Geumok, but she didn't know.

As soon as I got home, I went into the bedroom and rummaged through the drawers. Thankfully I still had her business card. I called the number. As the phone rang I spat out the acacia gum I'd been chewing. I'd chewed it all the way home and it still had a hint of flavor. I couldn't get through. I texted her. *It's Huiae. Call me when you get this.*

I went back to the doctor two days later, but I still hadn't heard from Geumok. I tried calling again as I waited my turn. Her phone was turned off. The nurse called out, Ms. Kim Huiae, come on in. The doctor told me the follicles were looking great and asked me to return with my husband the next day. They would collect them as planned. Hope you have good dreams tonight, the doctor added. I said I would.

Again, Geumok wasn't anywhere to be seen in front of the station today. I took a deep breath before letting it out. Then I headed the opposite way. I went down the alley and climbed the small hill until I reached the corner market. I banged on Geumok's green metal gate. That was all I could do, as there was no bell. Hey, Geumok, I called, banging. Geumok. Are you home?

I pounded for a long time, and the sliding door to the corner market opened instead of the gate. You're going to make my store collapse, admonished an old woman, her white hair combed back. Do you know Geumok, young lady? I said I was her friend. That can't be, she muttered. I'm sorry? I asked, taken aback, and the old woman said, You look at least ten years younger than her.

She invited me to wait in the store. She had thought it odd that she hadn't seen Geumok in more than ten days, but then she had finally bumped into her the previous night. It looked like she was coming back after a trip, the old woman said, and she'll be home today. I sat in the chair the old woman offered and was surprised. It was heated even though it was only September. This chair's so warm, I said. I keep it warm all year round, the old woman said. Even in the middle of summer? Yeah.

I thought I would get too hot sitting there, but that wasn't the case. I felt comforted. *It's nice to sit in a warm chair even when it's not cold,* I thought. I looked out the sliding glass door. People walked past the large gingko tree out front. I was watching the tree when the door slid open and a man with dyed yellow hair walked in.

The old woman glanced at him and whispered to me, Jin Ramen. And indeed, he bought a five-pack of Jin Ramen. When a tall woman stopped in, the old woman said, Homerun Ball and Bacchus. And indeed, the woman bought a packet of Homerun Ball and two bottles of Bacchus. When a bearded man opened the sliding door, I reflexively glanced at the old woman, who looked up at him but didn't say anything. And what about him? I asked, unable to wait. How would I know? she said grumpily. I laughed out loud without meaning to. The bearded man glanced at me while he selected his beverage: orange juice.

When he left, the old woman turned toward me. I initially thought Geumok ran off without paying rent, she said. But I knew she wouldn't do something like that. I told her she was right, that Geumok would never do a thing like that. So why did you come over without giving her a call? asked the old woman. Did you wrong her somehow? It did feel like I had wronged her somehow, so I told the old woman she was right.

The old woman stared at me, then tapped my chair. So you sit here and reflect, and when she comes you tell her you're sorry. I said I would.

Around the time the edges of the gingko leaves started to blend into the darkness, we heard the metal gate rattle. Go on, the old woman said, lightly squeezing my hand.

Geumok, I called, and Geumok jumped and turned her head. Her eyes darted all around. What's wrong? I asked, and she said it was nothing. But she tugged me in by the hand and quickly locked the gate behind us. We went down the stone steps without speaking. Only after we entered her place did I manage to open my mouth. Is something wrong? Geumok said no and turned on the light. Where have you been? I asked. Geumok didn't answer, then hung her jacket on a hanger and said something shocking. I went away with my boyfriend.

You have a boyfriend? Yeah. Why haven't you told me? I didn't have a chance. Where did you go? Incheon, we went fishing and ate raw fish. You know how to fish? Of course. I sat on the floor and watched her change out of her clothes. Are you telling the truth? I asked. Yes, I swear, she said. Now in comfortable clothes, she sat across from me. She said she had nothing to eat at home, let alone drink. I'm sorry, she said. I told her it was fine, that I had to get going soon anyway. Okay, she said, and stopped talking.

A brief silence stretched between us. I stared at Geumok's face as she looked silently down at the floor. Geumok, I blurted out. How was Incheon? She looked up. It was good. So you went fishing—did you catch anything? Yeah, it was as big as your arm, Huiae. My arms are still sore from pulling it out, she said, massaging her arm playfully. Did you eat it? I asked. Eat what? The fish, I said. Hey, do you think all I do is eat? Geumok asked, laughing. I laughed, too.

Then I said, fifteen-year-old Geumok couldn't even kill an ant. Geumok stopped laughing and looked at me. I was starting to feel uncomfortable when she finally spoke. Well, Huiae, she said. I nodded encouragingly. That was a long time ago, she said.

My legs were starting to cramp. I massaged my calves and told her I should get going. I'm sorry I can't see you out, Geumok said. I told her it was fine. But, Geumok, I said as I put my shoes on, next time, when you go on a trip or something, can you let me know? Yeah, she said. I stood up and looked at her. Somehow she looked shorter than when I'd first seen her on the street. As she said goodbye to me, I realized what it was. The cross that should have been hanging on the wall behind her was gone.

❊

The day after my eggs were retrieved, I packed a few things. My husband kept trying to convince me out of it, wanting me to rest at home this Chuseok. I told him I was feeling okay and that he shouldn't fret. Only after we argued did he concede that I should do as I pleased. I placed my socks on top of my things and zipped up my overnight bag. I knew what would happen if I didn't go to my father-in-law's house. Next Chuseok, and five years into the future, he would talk about how lonely he had been that one Chuseok. I wasn't sure I could listen to that over and over again.

We arrived in time for dinner. I smelled food cooking when the door swung open. Father, did you cook? I asked, taken aback. It had always fallen on me to cook after my mother-in-law passed away three years earlier. I headed into the kitchen to discover that he had already made toran guk.

I told my father-in-law that I would wash up, then dragged my husband into the room we stayed in. You told him we're doing IVF? I demanded once I closed the door. He didn't answer. When did you tell him? My husband said he'd told his father yesterday. That he'd had to say something because he wanted me to rest after the egg retrieval. I tried to calm down, but I couldn't speak for a while. Then let's pretend that I don't know that he knows, I managed. Chastened, my husband nodded.

I acted as though I wasn't aware of anything. I was surprised and apologetic when my husband volunteered to do the dishes and when my father-in-law personally cut melon for dessert. I pretended I didn't hear when my father-in-law almost brought up the topic of babies before trailing off. With my defenses up like that, I was exhausted by the time my father-in-law retired to bed. The bottle of lotion I picked up after washing my face felt like lead.

My husband had been quiet all night, and he maintained his silence when we were alone in our room. That was his way of telling me he was mad. He refused to speak until I figured out why he was angry and apologized for that precise thing. I tried to pinpoint when he'd gotten mad but gave up; I didn't have the energy to think. I took my medication and lay down. The blankets smelled musty. Though I'd expected to toss and turn all night, I quickly fell into deep slumber.

When I woke up, it was the middle of the night. My husband was asleep next to me. I went to the kitchen and filled the kettle to the brim. After the procedure I found myself constantly parched. I waited for the water to boil and glanced at the desktop calendar on the kitchen table. The fertilized egg would be implanted in two days. But there was a blue circle around September 2. Underneath, in small letters, was the word *family*.

What was September 2? There hadn't been any other family gatherings this month because of Chuseok. Everyone's birthday was in the winter, too. I mindlessly flipped to the previous month. Many more blue circles in August. Circles came one after another on the fourth and fifth weeks. I studied them, then slowly turned to the previous page. And again.

And again. The blue circles paraded on. My eyes welled. I thought I knew what those circles indicated. They had started even before we'd opted for artificial insemination.

In the taxi, I called Geumok. She picked up after a series of rings. Were you asleep? I asked. No, Geumok said, her voice still sleepy. Can I come over? I asked. Now? she asked. When I said yes, she told me to come on over. I hung up and told the driver to take me to a different address.

The green metal gate was already ajar, propped open by a rock. I removed the rock and went downstairs to knock on the front door. I rapped twice lightly, then twice harder. The door opened. Huiae, you're in your pajamas, Geumok said when she saw me. I looked down and discovered that I was.

I took off my shoes and went inside. Geumok stopped smiling and sat next to me. She sat quietly until I could speak. My head feels like it's going to split open, I said finally. She got up.

I thought she was going to get me some pills, but she opened up the small table. Then she came over with the pot, the old pot she used to make soup, to boil noodles, or to cook tteokbokki. I made this when you called me, she said. You have to eat something before you take any meds.

I opened the lid and found steamed egg. I spooned up a bit, causing white steam to curl up. I tried a bite. It was soft, warm. I spooned it silently and ate, then clapped with my spoon. Geumok laughed.

We laughed together, then began talking, slowly. We talked for a long time, and we took long breaks. When one of us spoke, the other didn't say a word until she was done. We looked into the other's eyes, demonstrating with our entire bodies that we were listening intently. We were moving past something together as we continued to talk. Slowly, but toward a clear direction, moving past time that swelled gently, that lacked sharp edges. For the first time ever, we were reaching a destination we longed for.

Go Sleep at Home

Jo, you got yourself a new habit since I saw you, I said. What habit? asked Jo. Looking around everywhere, I said. Oh, that, Jo said, but didn't elaborate. I didn't ask any further. I knew he would just make stuff up. Jo was the best liar among everyone I knew.

Once, I asked, Jo, why do you put your socks under your pillow? and his answer to that had also been Oh, that. When I asked again, frustrated by his nonexplanation, he said it was because of a house fire. That when he was a boy, his house caught fire while he was asleep. He'd had to dash out in the winter cold, and when he'd looked down, he was barefoot.

So this is how I lose my toes, Jo had thought gravely. After that, he said, I feel settled only when my socks are under my pillow. Once I heard that, I stopped needling him about his weird habit.

Another time I asked him why he had two toothbrushes in his bathroom. Jo said, Oh, that. One's for the morning and one's for at night. He looked so earnest that I just said, Oh, okay.

Only a long time later did I learn that Jo never lived through a house fire or used different toothbrushes for morning and night. Why do you lie about that stuff? I demanded, but Jo said again, Oh, that, and started to make something up, so I decided to stop asking. After that, whenever Jo started a sentence with *Oh, that,* I didn't ask for details. Then he, too, would stop talking.

But this time Jo started to elaborate. Kim Jaehyeon's gone missing, he said. He downed his drink.

Kim Jaehyeon's gone missing? I stared at him in shock. Kim Jaehyeon was the name of the crested gecko Jo had had for eight years.

Last weekend, it was so hot that Jo had opened the window in the middle of the night, half asleep. A mosquito had entered the room and buzzed by Jo's ear. Irritated, Jo had sprayed bug repellent all over the room, only to belatedly become concerned for Kim Jaehyeon. He moved the gecko to the bathroom. There was nowhere else to put him, since he lived in a studio apartment. Jo had cleaned the bathroom the day before, so he let Kim Jaehyeon out to roam. I'll move you back in your tank after I clean the room in the morning, he said. But the next morning, when he opened the bathroom door, Kim Jaehyeon was nowhere to be found. Only the half-open drain cover greeted Jo.

Are you okay? I asked stupidly, and Jo drew a line on the table with his index finger. What are you doing? I asked, and he replied, This is the plumbing. I got a copy of the building's plumbing plans. I opened everything up but he wasn't there. Jo's finger pointed out select locations on the table. Not here, not there. Nowhere.

Jo kept sinking into his own thoughts. Any time I said something or people entered or left the bar, he'd look around in a panic, like he was searching for Kim Jaehyeon. Like he wasn't sure why he was sitting there.

Every time he did that, I had to stop myself from saying what I really wanted to. *Jo, you didn't react like this back then. You were fine.* Useless words like that. The bottle emptied swiftly as we got quieter. My head was starting to pound, and I asked if he was lonely. Yeah, Jo said. Do you want to sleep over? I asked. He said he was fine, that everything was fine, and that we should get going.

❉

I lowered my chair as soon as I got to work. I cleaned my desk with a wet wipe, then poured a little drinking water into the succulent. The plant was there when I started the job; nobody knew who had brought it over or when. This was my first post-college job, working as a security guard in a mixed-use high-rise building.

We were divided into three teams on two shifts. I was on for two days, got a day off, then did two nights, then got a night off. At first it was torture to sit in the same place for twelve hours straight. The most difficult part was killing time.

At least time passed quickly during the day shift, with all kinds of tasks to do. The problem was the night shift. From midnight to six in the morning, most of the residents were in their homes, which made time inch by slower than a mule hauling waterlogged cotton.

All kinds of thoughts popped into your head when you tried to kill time. Mostly things that had happened a very long time ago. The last time I was organizing packages, I found the name of the kid I sat next to in elementary school. For a week, when things were slow, I thought only about that kid. We had been close for a long time, and I couldn't remember why we drifted apart. I recalled getting gummy vitamins from his mom, who owned a pharmacy, and how he gave me impossible-to-flip ttakji for my ninth birthday, but I just couldn't remember that one thing.

On the third day, I went to a snack bar for lunch and finally remembered what had happened. It was all because of tteokbokki. One day, we had tteokbokki for school lunch, and we tucked into it more eagerly than any other day. We had classes the rest of the afternoon and were leaving the classroom after the last bell when our teacher said to him, You know you have food on your face? I realized only then that tteokbokki sauce was smeared on his mouth and cheek.

He swiped his mouth with the back of his hand, then, a few steps later, shouted at me. You sit next to me and you didn't tell me? I don't want to talk to you from now on. Coincidentally the whole class was made to switch seats the very next day, and that really became the last time I spoke to him.

Four more days of thinking later, I remembered that wasn't true. Sometime later, I bumped into him at the bus stop. I didn't know you were really going to stop talking to me, he said. I told him that wasn't it, that after we changed seats I didn't have an excuse to talk to him. And that really was the last time. I was stupid. I wanted to apologize now, although years had passed.

When half of what I talked about started with *Jo, remember that time . . . ?* Jo told me I should get a new job. I hadn't even been on the job for two months. As if he was any better. Around that time, Jo had a gig checking for defects in plates and cups, which he loathed. He claimed he'd started noticing defects in everything. He couldn't stand a scratch on his phone or a crease on his bag. Thankfully he quit that job soon after realizing he would immediately use any money he earned on new replacements.

Jo called as I was about to get off work. Kim Jaehyeon was here the whole time, he said, sounding excited. I pulled my phone off my ear to check who was calling me. It was Jo all right. So he was home the whole time? I asked. No, no. In the building. The guy upstairs says he saw him. And? I asked. He asked the landlady to call an exterminator because he couldn't catch him. I just found out because she texted to say that an exterminator's coming. I called her right back, but she says she can't cancel the appointment because she promised the guy upstairs. So I had to tell her the gecko was mine. And then she flipped out.

Why are you telling me this? I interrupted, unable to stop myself. Come with me, Jo said. Where? Upstairs, he said. She says I should go talk to the guy myself. I was hoping you'd come with me. I'm at work right now, I said, pretending to be regretful. Jo said he would wait. I hesitated, and Jo added, Please.

The door to unit 501 flung open the instant we rang the bell. The guy was in an undershirt, his sweaty hair stuck to his forehead. Yes? he asked, looking from me to Jo, his hand on the doorknob. I heard you found a gecko yesterday, Jo said. Oh, you're the exterminators! The guy opened the door wider. I detected a whiff of something musty. No, I said, grabbing Jo by the arm, he lives downstairs and he's the owner of the gecko.

The gecko has an owner? The man's voice rose in surprise. I tensed my grip on Jo's arm. Of course, I said. He's practically this guy's family. I wasn't exaggerating. Whenever Jo told someone about his family, he said it was his father, himself, and Kim Jaehyeon. If someone asked, Did you say Kim Jaehyeon? Jo would just say, Yes, and people who knew his personality didn't ask anything further, figuring there was some story or other.

Could you show us where you saw the gecko? I asked. That's going to be a problem, the guy said, pulling the door closer toward him. My place is a mess right now. Jo piped up: Well, my friend here works for a cleaning company. We'll clean your place for free. You know how expensive it is to hire cleaners. And you'll feel better once I take the gecko away.

Then you don't even have to get the exterminators to come. The guy thought about it for a second with his hand still on the doorknob, then told us to come in.

I elbowed Jo in the ribs as we took our shoes off. He ignored me. The guy's studio was a disaster, buried under all sorts of things. It smelled horrible from all the take-out containers piled up everywhere, and clothes were strewn across the floor. There would be no point in calling an exterminator with this mess, Jo murmured to me. Do you want to step outside while we clean? I asked the guy. He shook his head. Am I supposed to just trust you? Then do you have some disposable gloves we can use? asked Jo.

I pulled on the disposable gloves the guy handed us and opened the window. Then I began collecting all the empty plastic bottles in one place. Don't you usually bring your own supplies? the guy asked me. Usually yes, Jo replied, but this wasn't planned, so. Behind the guy's back Jo mouthed, *Sorry*, to me.

Where did you see Kim Jaehyeon? Jo asked the guy. Before the guy could ask, I told him that Kim Jaehyeon was the gecko's name. On the sink, the guy said. He was eating leftover cheese pizza. Kim Jaehyeon doesn't eat cheese pizza, protested Jo. Kim Jaehyeon seemed to like it, the guy said. I turned to look back at the guy. Nobody had ever called Kim Jaehyeon by name from the start.

Instead of responding, Jo searched the sink and under the closet. He hopped on a storage bin to check the inside of the light fixture. While he did that I picked clothes off the floor. I found a few long-sleeved shirts even though it was the middle of summer.

Oddly, I kept finding black hair ties. The guy's hair was shaggy but not long enough to tie up. Every time I found a hair tie I slid it on my wrist. While we worked, the guy sat against the wall and played a game on his phone.

It was already ten at night, but we hadn't even gone through half the studio. The guy put his phone down and asked if we were hungry. Would you like some ramyeon? Jo told him we weren't done yet. Come back tomorrow, the guy said. It's just that I'm hungry. He filled a pot with water. Can we really come back tomorrow? Jo asked. You won't call the exterminator, will you? Yeah, sure, the guy said, surprisingly agreeable. Only then, after two hours of cleaning, did we sit down.

Because of the pile of dishes in the sink, we used paper cups as serving bowls. The ramyeon he made was way too salty. I don't have a bigger pot, the guy said after the first bite. I must not have used enough water. I told him it was fine. The guy's name was Jeongu. He went to the nearby university, but he was taking some time off. Which meant that he went to Jo's alma mater. I glanced at Jo, but because he didn't say anything, I stayed mum, too.

Mid-meal, Jeongu asked what I had on my wrist. Oh, I found these while cleaning, I forgot. I took the hair ties off and gave them to Jeongu. Deep red marks were imprinted on my wrist. Jeongu put his chopsticks down. He rubbed his nose with the back of his hand and opened up to us.

See, a month ago I broke up with my girlfriend, he said. I usually keep things pretty clean, but after that day I didn't want to do *anything*, forget about cleaning. I wouldn't eat a thing all day until the middle of the night, when I'd order in, then drink by myself. Oh, a while ago I signed up for Watcha. It recommends five movies a week, and so I watched them all, but weirdly the recommendations keep getting further away from what I like. But I still watch them all. And then last night, I saw a really great movie for the first time. So I picked myself up, put down the crap I was eating, and decided to tackle the dishes. But that thing was there. It was long and dark, and it was wiggling on the pizza from the day before, and it was so creepy. I was practically in tears. And I'm not usually like that.

I glanced at Jo. I could tell he was barely keeping it together. Jeongu didn't notice and kept talking. Anyway, it was really rough, but it's nice to eat and chat with you guys. I haven't done that in a while. Why did you break up with your girl? Jo asked out of the blue. That's the thing I don't understand, Jeongu said, his face crumpling like he'd bitten down on a pebble. I keep asking, but she won't tell me.

Before we left, Jeongu asked Jo when he would be back tomorrow. I'll come up after breakfast, Jo said. We left Jeongu's apartment and walked down a flight. It's late, you can stay over, Jo told me. I hadn't been there since we broke up. I tensed for some reason while Jo tapped the passcode to unlock the door. But when the door swung open and I spotted the familiar interior, I felt instantly at ease.

The only thing that had changed in Jo's apartment was Kim Jaehyeon's tank. I'd never seen it empty and unlit. I placed a hand on the glass wall of the tank. Whenever I did that Kim Jaehyeon would scurry toward my hand. I lifted my hand off and realized I'd left a hazy imprint, though it quickly disappeared.

I turned around to find Jo drinking water. So I work for a cleaning company, huh? I asked. Jo put the cup down and put his hands together in contrition. I just had to check with my own eyes, he said. I'm sorry. I told him it was fine, that I wanted some water, too. He handed me his cup. I downed the rest of the water. I was so thirsty, maybe because of that salty ramyeon.

I came out of the bathroom after washing up to find Jo already lying on a mat on the floor, covered by a blanket. Get up, I'll sleep on the floor. I shook him by the shoulder. I'm sleeping, he said, his eyes closed. Don't wake me up. In the end, I dried my hair and lay in his bed.

Not long after I turned off the lights, I heard crickets chirping. Kim Jaehyeon's food. I'd sometimes heard chirping when we were together, but I'd never heard so many of them at the same time. I thought Jo was sleeping, but he said, I'm going to let them all go if I don't find Kim Jaehyeon in a month.

I looked down at him. He was turned the other way, his arm tucked under his head. I noticed that there was only one pillow. He must have thrown mine out. I lay on my back and looked up at the ceiling. I wasn't sure I would be able to fall asleep because of the chirping, but sleep came instantly.

The rustling woke me up. When I opened my eyes, I saw Jo opening the plastic liner of a cereal box in the dark. You can turn the light on, I said, and the room turned bright. Jo took out a bowl from the cupboard and made me some, too. Frosted cornflakes with a splash of milk. He still ate cereal every morning. I finished my cereal and lifted the bowl to drink the leftover milk. It was so sweet that it chased away any drowsiness.

Jo said he would walk me to the bus stop. Didn't you say you were going back upstairs? I asked. I'll go with you. Jo told me it was fine, that I had done more than enough yesterday. It's my day off and I don't have anything else to do, I said. Then thanks, Jo said with a shrug.

We headed upstairs. But Jeongu didn't come to the door even though we leaned on the bell. A very long time later, he finally opened the door. He looked like he'd been asleep. His hair was a mess and his eyes were barely open.

Were you sleeping? We can come back later, I said. Jeongu waved away my words. That's not important, he said. I think I'm going to have to call the exterminators after all. Sorry. Why, what happened? Jo pressed. I went to bed last night and heard bug noises, Jeongu said. I figured it was coming from outside, but then I remembered I live on the fifth floor. I turned on all the lights and searched and searched, and I found a camel cricket! I was up all night. So I think I'm going to have to bring in exterminators. Sorry about that. Look, said Jo calmly. Why don't we go inside and talk? Jeongu hesitated, then let us in.

Did you catch the cricket? Jo asked. It was jumping all around, how could I? Jeongu protested. I managed to get it outside. Jeongu didn't seem to want to even think about it. It must have gotten in somehow, Jo said firmly. If you call the exterminators Kim Jaehyeon will die. Those chemicals are fatal to geckos, you know. You promised me yesterday. You can't call them. I stared at Jo. Had he ever been this serious about anything? Jeongu seemed taken aback. I'll go wash up now, so go ahead and look for him, he said, and went into the bathroom.

I shot Jo a look. Are you serious? I hissed. Jo had obviously let crickets out yesterday, along with the others. I can't let him starve, can I? Jo said, quickly adding, Don't tell.

With Jeongu's permission, Jo removed everything from the bookcase and the cupboards. Even Jeongu helped in the search and finally agreed to wait to call the exterminators. While the two of them looked for Kim Jaehyeon, I mopped the floor. Halfway through I flipped the rag over; it was shockingly dirty. Look at this, I said, holding the rag up high. Jo checked the bottom of his socks. I checked the bottom of mine, too, but they were already filthy.

For a while we kept pulling things apart and putting them back together. We searched the bookcase and the cupboards, of course, and even the closet and the bathroom, but we couldn't find Kim Jaehyeon. We just found two more black hair ties—a total of five, counting the ones I found yesterday. She always said she didn't have anything to tie her hair with, Jeongu said, and shoved them all in a drawer.

Once we were done, we hung up laundry to dry and turned on the AC. We brought out a low table to the middle of the room and sat down, the scent of laundry detergent gently perfuming the air around us. Jeongu took beer out of the fridge. On Jo's suggestion, we had ordered pizza. What do you think? Jeongu asked. Doesn't it make sense that Kim Jaehyeon would have wanted to eat it? Jo didn't answer but picked up a second slice. I told Jeongu it was good. I've been getting pizza only from here since I moved in, Jeongu said. With that, silence settled over us. Jo, who had searched under the closet right until the pizza arrived, ate without uttering a word.

Jeongu broke the silence. I was drunk and lying in bed, and I heard someone singing. I guess it was you. Jo stared at Jeongu. How was it? How was what? My singing. Jeongu thought it over. It wasn't bad. More like Lee So Ra than Park Hyo Shin. I laughed. Jo told me that wasn't funny.

Jo said that he, too, had lain in bed, staring at the ceiling, at one point in his life. That was when the name Kim Jaehyeon came to me, he said, cracking open a second beer. Kim

Jaehyeon hadn't always been Kim Jaehyeon. He hadn't had a name for more than six months. When Jo was in junior high, his friend had asked him to watch the gecko while he went on a family trip, then hadn't come back for him. That was how Jo had ended up with the pet. After growing apart from that friend, Jo had done nothing but lie in bed.

One day, he was lying in bed as always, when the gecko he'd thought was in the tank climbed up the wall and onto the ceiling, before falling on his face. Jo had grabbed his nose and run to the bathroom. His nose was fine. But neither the pain nor his miffed feelings subsided. The gecko was on his ceiling when he went back in his room. Jo put the gecko in the tank and glared at him. And he decided to give him the worst name in the world. *Kim Jaehyeon*. His homeroom teacher's name. Later he would regret naming him in that manner, but by then no other name suited the gecko.

While Jeongu listened intently to Jo's story, I slathered hot sauce all over my pizza and focused on eating. I'd already heard this story a million times. What I wondered every time wasn't about Kim Jaehyeon but why Jo had felt compelled to do nothing but stare at the ceiling at that point in his life. But I didn't ask that question this time, either.

We devoured the entire pizza. Before we left, Jo thanked Jeongu. He added that Jeongu should call him if he saw Kim Jaehyeon, even in the middle of the night. Sure, Jeongu said easily, now fully apprised of everything about Kim Jaehyeon. We left and headed to the bus stop. The heat wave was unrelenting, the night air damp and hot. We walked in silence.

When we got to the bus stop Jo thanked me, too. No problem, I said.

The screen at the stop showed that my bus was eleven minutes away. You don't have to stay here, I said. Go home. I'll wait with you, Jo said, settling on the bench. I sat next to him. I was looking at how Jo's T-shirt stuck to his back when he asked, What are you doing tomorrow? Working, of course, I said. It's been exactly two years, he said. You remembered? I asked. Yeah. And then we were quiet.

When the bus pulled up, I said, See you soon. I took a seat and looked out to find Jo waving.

❋

I opened my two-tiered lunch box. The upper level held neatly sliced chicken breast, bite-sized broccoli pieces, and cherry tomatoes. The lower level contained brown rice. The same meal I'd brought for night shifts for the last two years. In the winter I packed sweet potato instead of brown rice.

At first, I didn't eat anything on night shifts. I'd been focused on staying toned in my college days, so I wasn't used to eating so late at night. But staying awake a few nights a week on an empty stomach made my gut ache. So at one in the morning I began eating the food I brought from home. Then I didn't gain weight and my stomach didn't hurt, either. I stocked chicken breast I ordered in bulk online in the freezer.

I was about to pick up a cherry tomato when the automatic doors slid open. I stood to greet the resident but sat down again when I realized nobody was there. Even so, I said, Hello. From time to time, in the middle of the night, the doors opened even when nobody was there. On nights like those the doors malfunctioned precisely two times. I thought it meant that someone was coming in and then leaving. So I started greeting the doors. The first time I said, Hello, and the second time I said, Goodbye.

Then, strangely, good things would happen. The person coming to relieve me, who was always five minutes late, would suddenly show up on time, or I'd open a bottle of Vita500 and see the words *Free drink* printed on the inside of the cap. Little lucky things like that. *This person must have been a good person when they were alive,* I thought as I ate some broccoli. I wondered how Jo was doing. Was he still looking for Kim Jaehyeon? I was about to text him but decided it was too late at night.

The problem was that I couldn't stop thinking about Jo and Kim Jaehyeon even after my shift, even after my nap. *Jo, what's going on with Kim Jaehyeon?* I finally texted him. He texted me back a while later. *I'm at Jeongu's. He said he heard something in the cupboards.* I was about to respond when my phone buzzed again. *Wanna come?*

I opened the front door and the smell of kimchi jjigae hit me. We haven't found Kim Jaehyeon, Jeongu reported even before I took my shoes off. We pulled everything out from all the cupboards, but he wasn't there, he added.

Worried, I looked around for Jo. He was crouched in the corner, scooping rice out of the cooker. Perfect timing, he said when he saw me. You'll have some, right? I said I would.

Jeongu had just made the jjigae. Everyone asks for my recipe when I make it on retreats, he boasted. I tried some. What do you think? Jeongu asked. It's good, Jo and I answered at the same time, inhaling the stew. You're eating too fast, Jo told Jeongu. The two of them seemed to have gotten a lot closer in the last few days. Jo had stopped using honorifics, and he found the scissors when Jeongu was looking around for them. I know where everything is now that I've combed through the entire place, Jo said, and informed me that he'd been coming over every single day. Every single day? I asked, surprised, and Jo said he kept getting the feeling that Kim Jaehyeon was here somewhere.

Jeongu suggested we watch a movie on his laptop. He told us to pick a movie while he did the dishes. We chose one the algorithm predicted Jeongu would rate as five stars. It should be good since it's supposed to be five stars, I said, and Jo nodded. We propped the laptop on the table and sat against the wall, Jeongu next to Jo next to me. The movie was about monsters who killed people the moment they made a noise. Because of that the characters kept silent. They tiptoed about, trying not to snap even a twig.

The movie ended with the main character killing the monsters using high-frequency radio waves, and Jo flopped down on his back. That was so nerve-racking! he yelled. I copied him: That was so nerve-racking! I told you, Jeongu said sheepishly, it doesn't recommend movies I actually like. If you guys keep yelling the downstairs neighbor's going to come up to complain. *I'm* the downstairs neighbor, Jo reminded him. We'd be quieter if you tell us that those monsters are coming, I said. Time for you two to go home, Jeongu said.

Before leaving, I used the bathroom. As I washed my hands, I noticed the drain cover was missing. Next to it was a plate of chopped banana.

An elegant elevator speaks volumes about you. I read the first sentence out loud as I posted the notice in the elevator at work. It had sounded pretty good when I'd read it to myself, but it sounded stupid when I heard it out loud. That morning, the maintenance office had told us to post a notice about new elevator designs in each elevator.

There was a total of four designs. Over the next week, residents could put a sticker on their favorite design, and the one with the most votes would be selected. Among them there was even a design that was apparently used in Burj Khalifa in Dubai. I studied that picture closely, then put a sticker under it.

I got a text as I emerged from the elevator. It was Jeongu. *Hyeong, can you bring beer when you come over?* I said I would. Lately I had been going to Jeongu's a few times a week. His place was between work and my place, and more importantly, Jo was always there.

We developed some ground rules as we started to meet up regularly. Everyone took turns paying for alcohol. Everyone would need to help the moment Kim Jaehyeon was spotted. Each of us had assigned positions in the event Kim Jaehyeon appeared. Jeongu would be by the balcony doors, Jo would be in front of the bathroom, and I would be at the sink. We couldn't get hammered. Jo had decreed that last rule because one time Jeongu got sloshed and talked incessantly about his ex-girlfriend until he cried. Jo had to talk Jeongu down for more than two hours. And we determined who would clean up with a game of rock-paper-scissors. I'd never once lost.

Hyeong, how can you never lose? Jeongu said after he'd traded doing the dishes with Jo for two weeks in a row. Now that I think of it, I haven't lost at rock-paper-scissors since last summer, I said. Jeongu told me to stop being ridiculous. But I wasn't being ridiculous. I hadn't lost at rock-paper-scissors ever since I started greeting the automatic doors that opened to no one. But I moved on, not sure how to explain that.

We also ended up with a group chat. When work was slow, I texted with Jeongu. Usually Jeongu started it and I answered, and most of the time we were deciding what to eat. Jo rarely checked our messages.

Sometimes Jeongu would text me separately with an invitation to play a game where you made coffee and sold it. He had met his ex while working at a café, and he did the same job even in a game.

Hurry up, Jeongu texted now. I didn't respond.

A little later, the kid who lived in 501, who ran out of the elevator every evening in a tae kwon do uniform, said, Hello! Aren't you supposed to be in school? I asked, and the kid yelled, Summer break started last week! and dashed out. Lucky, I murmured as the doors closed.

I headed to Jeongu's with beer and found him smoking outside. Hyeong, you're here! Yeah, I said. I just heard you work at a security company, not a cleaning company, he said. I was caught off guard and was about to make excuses, then changed my mind and apologized. That's okay, Jeongu replied placidly. I don't think lies like that are necessarily bad. Why not? I asked. Why aren't those bad? Jeongu turned his head to the side to let out a plume of smoke. Well, because I know how hard you tried to find Kim Jaehyeon. And anyway, you did clean my place for me. Jeongu stubbed his cigarette out and grabbed the beer. Come on, let's go inside, he said. It's hot out here.

Jo reminded us that today was Jungbok. Chicken is what we need on a day like this, he said. So we ordered fried chicken. It felt amazing to sip beer in the cool apartment. I put my beer down and picked up a piece of chicken, when Jeongu said to me, Hyeong, you're a really good guy. Most people go for the leg or the wing. You're the only person who'd choose the neck first.

I told him I'd just grabbed what was on top. Still, you're a really good guy, Hyeong, he said. Yeah, Jo agreed. Instead of replying I ate the chicken neck. The bones were unusually prickly today and poked the roof of my mouth. I spat out the bones and said, I think I am, too. But they didn't seem to hear me.

When we were halfway through the chicken, Jeongu announced out of the blue, It's not a big deal that you don't work for a cleaning company. Once, when you weren't here, I asked

Jo if he'd gotten his heart broken before, he continued. And he said that it still hurt whenever he saw a photo studio. He said he used to like someone who owned a photo studio, and one day that person vanished without a word. So he waited out front every day and wrote letters and slipped them in through the door, and then he was so upset and angry that he even threw a rock through the glass. But he heard nothing, so he eventually moved on, but later he found out that— The owner had a terminal illness, I jumped in. He tricked you, too? Jeongu asked. Yeah. See, thank God *Christmas in August* was last week's recommended movie, or else I might never have realized, Jeongu said. I couldn't believe it, so I laughed instead of crying during the credits.

You're the idiots who believed the story, Jo said. If believing a story makes you an idiot, then the person who lied is worse, I found myself saying. For a long time, I would look intently at the owner of every photo studio I passed by.

Still, Hyeong, Jeongu said to me, I wish my girlfriend would tell me why she dumped me, even if she made something up. A moment later, he asked, Do you think she'll take me back? Jo and I answered in unison: No.

When things quieted down after everyone went to work in the morning, I called the elevator. The doors slid open. I counted the stickers on the Burj Khalifa design: thirty-six. Five more than yesterday, but it was still trailing its neighbor by two votes.

In the last few days, I had been checking the sticker tally any time I had a moment. After lunch, when things were slow, and whenever I was curious, I would get up from my chair and press the elevator call button. I kept thinking about the elevators even though I knew they weren't that important. That would come to an end today. Tomorrow was the last day of the vote, and it was also my day off. Before I got off the elevator, I took three stickers from the other designs and stuck them below Burj Khalifa.

Back at work after my day off, I felt anxious on my way up to the maintenance office. I clocked in and asked as nonchalantly as possible, What happened with the elevators? The maintenance office worker looked at me and asked, What elevators? Didn't the design get decided on yesterday? I asked. Oh, that. He flipped through the pile of documents next to him, his gestures revealing his annoyance. I waited patiently.

Looks like B won, the maintenance office worker said, finally landing on the correct document. B? Not C? I asked. C came in third place, he said. You know, B was the only gold design. Older people like that color. Then he said, Oh, right, stopping me in my tracks. We got a complaint. You greeted the resident in 901 while seated. I racked my brain but couldn't remember ever saying hello while remaining in my chair. I'll be sure to stand, I promised. I went back to my post and felt like eating something spicy. I texted the group chat that I wanted to eat tteokbokki. Jo responded immediately: *Me too.*

At Jeongu's, we called in our tteokbokki order and brought out the low table. I think Kim Jaehyeon's gone, Jo said as he sat across from me. None of the food has been eaten. But then Jeongu said, I didn't say this before because I wasn't positive, but sometimes, when I turn off the lights, I hear him.

So we turned off the lights and lay quietly on the floor until the food was delivered. I didn't hear anything, only the faint whir of the AC. I nearly fell asleep a few times. We all jumped when the delivery guy rang the bell.

We ate the tteokbokki, and Jo said he was going to let all the crickets go. Already? I asked, and Jo said it had already been a month. You should still come hang out, Jeongu said. Sure, Jo said. And don't forget it's your turn to do the dishes today, Jeongu reminded Jo. We had done rock-paper-scissors the moment the food arrived. Jeongu and I had flashed paper. Jo had gone with rock.

❊

Hello, I said, standing to greet the resident in 901. After the complaint I greeted him with care, but he never responded. I sat back down and my shirt squeezed my midsection. I'd recently gained a good amount of weight. At Jeongu's I'd been eating too much fattening food that I normally didn't touch. The guy who clocked in on the next shift told me I seemed happier.

So I signed up for a gym membership. Once he'd freed the crickets, Jo stopped looking for Kim Jaehyeon, and I'd started going to the gym after work instead of Jeongu's. Nine out of ten times when I checked my phone on my way out of the gym, I found a message from Jeongu. *What are you two doing? I'm bored.* Sometimes he sent pictures of himself eating alone. It was torture to even look at those pictures when I was starving after working out. Jeongu texted often, but Jo never reached out first.

I was starting to feel put out by Jo when, one day, his name popped up on my phone. I stepped outside to pick up. Did you see my text? Jo asked as soon as I answered. No, not yet. What happened? Jeongu said he opened his eyes this morning and found Kim Jaehyeon on the ceiling, he said. So he got him? I asked. No, Jo said. What? He vanished, Jo explained. The bathroom door was closed, along with the door to the balcony and the window, and he wasn't by the sink. That means Kim Jaehyeon was with us the whole time. Jo told me he was on his way to Jeongu's. I said I would stop by after work. Thanks, Jo said.

Jeongu's place was a wreck when I got there. Jo and Jeongu were collapsed in the middle of the chaos. Where's Kim Jaehyeon? I demanded as soon as I entered. He's not here, Jeongu said. Jo didn't speak. We tore everything apart, but he's not here, Jeongu repeated, and lay back down on the floor. I don't even know anymore. It's fine, now that we know he's alive, Jo said. I'm done with this.

It looks like you just moved in, I said. Did you eat yet? Still lying on the floor, Jeongu shook his head. I do feel like jjajangmyeon, now that you're talking about moving, he said. I told him it was on me, to order whatever he wanted. Jeongu sprang up. One second, he said, and rummaged through a drawer. I have a frequent customer card from a Chinese restaurant. If we're lucky we could get a tangsuyuk for free.

Eventually Jeongu found a coupon the size of a business card. The red card was printed with the name *The Forbidden City*, but out of ten boxes only five had been stamped. I thought I had a lot, but we're nowhere close, Jeongu said. Then Jo said he had the same coupon at home and would bring it over. Maybe they'll let us combine them, he said.

But the coupon Jo brought back had only two stamps. We gave up and ordered jjajangmyeon for three and a plate of tangsuyuk. I can't believe both of you stopped coming over, Jeongu said, snapping his wooden chopsticks apart. I started going to the gym, I said. Jo said, Oh, that— and both Jeongu and I cut him off and told him it was fine. Jo scowled and said he'd been sick. What? Jeongu said, looking panicked. Just a bad cold, Jo said. In the middle of the summer? Jeongu demanded. Why didn't you call me? I'm right upstairs. Just because, Jo said, helping himself to tangsuyuk. It was fine.

Afterward we did rock-paper-scissors for the dishes. The take-out dishes could be placed outside for the delivery guy to pick up, but we still had to wash the cups. Jo threw scissors. Jeongu did, too. I had gone with paper. Our hands hung in the air for a moment. You actually lost, Hyeong, Jeongu said to me, shocked. So I guess what you said last time was a lie, huh? I quickly pulled my hand back and did the dishes slowly on purpose. As I swiveled the sponge in one of the cups I realized what had gone wrong. Two days ago, on the night shift, the sliding doors had malfunctioned only once. I scrubbed the cup forcefully. It's going to be morning by the time you finish washing three cups, Jo said.

In line at a café after lunch, I heard the woman in front of me say to her friend, It's too cold for iced drinks now. Only then did I notice summer was over. I realized they'd stopped turning on the AC at work in the evenings. Back at my post, I took a sip of my iced coffee and regretted that I hadn't heeded the stranger's advice.

This morning, the remodeling of the elevators was fully completed. They were not at all to my taste. Whenever I rode in the elevator with its gold-painted doors and railing, I felt like a cheap present wrapped in gold foil. *I shouldn't think that,* I told myself, but would find myself ruminating on it even more.

I was set to go over to Jeongu's after work today. Last night, he had sent a picture to the group. The group chat hadn't been active in two weeks, not since Jo had texted, *I'm on my way*. The picture was of two Forbidden City coupons. I'd zoomed in and saw there were eight stamps on Jeongu's coupon and two on Jo's, for a total of ten. *I ordered twice without you,* Jeongu had texted. He'd suggested we eat the free tangsuyuk together since Jo and I had contributed to the collection of stamps. I'd texted, *I'll be there*. In the morning, I saw that Jo had said he'd be there, too.

Jeongu opened the door, and I set down the watermelon I'd brought. I was sweaty from lugging the big melon up five flights. Now I wished I had the iced coffee from earlier. What's with the watermelon? Jeongu tried to put it in the fridge, but it didn't fit, so he placed it in the corner of the room. We can't let summer go by without having watermelon, I said. But it turned out that I was the only one who hadn't had watermelon this summer. Jo had had some at a relative's wedding last week, and Jeongu had bought watermelon juice at a fresh fruit juice shop just yesterday.

We decided on the same dishes as last time: three jjajangmyeon, one large tangsuyuk. While Jeongu called our order in, I peered at the game Jo was playing on his phone. It was the same one Jeongu played. Weird, Jeongu said, looking over at us. They're not picking up. We called again on speaker. It rang and rang, then went to voicemail. It says on the coupon that it's open every day of the year, Jeongu said in frustration. Maybe they went under, Jo said. But I ordered from them yesterday, Jeongu said. We called ten minutes later, but nobody picked up. Only after Jo said, Let's just eat instant jjajangmyeon, did Jeongu let go of his phone.

Jo made five packets of instant jjajangmyeon. One isn't close to enough for one person, Jo said, and he was right. Even five packets weren't quite enough for the three of us. We cut into the watermelon. Jeongu didn't have a decent knife, so we struggled for a while with a small paring knife and scissors. We finally managed to crack it, and I gripped both sides and split it open. With a giant snap, pieces flew all around us. Good thing you've been working out, Jeongu said. Having spent all our energy trying to cut the watermelon, we dug straight into the fruit with spoons. It wasn't all that sweet or cool, but it wasn't bad.

As we ate, I told them all about the new elevators. Even the floor is gold? Jeongu asked. And the buttons? I told him everything was gold except for the black buttons. Makes me want to go ride that elevator, Jeongu said, and Jo laughed: I never heard anyone say they wanted to go somewhere just to ride the elevator. I'll go visit Hyeong and take a ride, Jeongu said, spooning up watermelon. You know, I'm really thankful to you both. If it weren't for you I'd still be lying on the floor, obsessing over my ex. I owe you so much. We raised you right, I said, and Jo laughed.

So there's something I've been meaning to ask, Jo said. What was Kim Jaehyeon doing when you saw him that last time? He was just staring down at me, Jeongu said. Without even moving? No, he was just blinking his eyes. Can you show me? Jo asked. I glanced at Jo. He looked serious, without a hint of a smile.

It won't look the same even if I show you, Jeongu said, laughing, but Jo was firm: I want to see it. Show me. Jeongu finally put his spoon down and blinked his eyes rapidly, twice. That was when I understood why Jo had asked. A crested gecko didn't have eyelids. Jo sprang to his feet. How long has it been? How long have you been lying that you saw Kim Jaehyeon? Did you lie about hearing something in the cupboards, too? Jeongu asked him what he was talking about. Jo stalked toward the door without a word. Asshole, Jeongu shouted at Jo. You're assholes! Both of you!

I caught up to Jo on the stairs. Did you know he was lying? Jo's voice rang out in the stairwell. No, not till now, I said. Jo stood there without speaking. Do you want me to stay with you? I asked. Do you want to get some fresh air? Jo shook his head. He went down the stairs, entered the code in his door, and walked into his apartment. The door closed firmly behind him. A moment later I continued down the stairs.

At the bus stop, I looked up at the screen. Eight minutes. I sat on the bench. Nobody was there, so I lay down. The inky sky was above me, without a single visible star. I felt like staying there like that until morning. Soon I heard the bus pull up, but I ignored it. I would lie here until I didn't feel like lying here anymore. I wouldn't go to work tomorrow. I wouldn't pack my lunch, I wouldn't go to the gym. I told myself these things resolutely as I let at least five buses go by. I was about to doze off when someone whispered, kindly, in my ear, Go sleep at home. Startled, I opened my eyes. I looked around, but nobody was there.

The Hibernating Guy

Now you're dead. You just keeled over. At home, in the middle of the living room. You'll hear the motor of the fridge running, your neighbor's door opening and closing. But you're not going to move at all, because you're dead. That's when she comes in.

She's wobbling. She's like a demon. The one who killed you. The kind of person who would sit on your dead belly and take a sip of gin. And then he enters.

He's gentle. He coaxes her off your body and gets her in bed. And then he's overcome by emotion and stands there in the kitchen, crying. He'll wake her up the next morning gently, like nothing's wrong. They'll have breakfast, they'll dance, and they'll drink triple shots of espresso. And then they'll leave and start things all over again. Murder, arson, muggings, terrible things.

And is that when I stand up and get revenge? I ask. I had been nibbling on a cookie as I listened to all this.

No. Remember, you're dead.

Then why am I in their house?

Your role, the director said, and paused to think, is atmospheric. You're there to set the mood.

For twenty-six shows, I lay still on the stage. My eyes were closed, but still, the lights were blinding. I lay on my back, listening to the demonic woman and the gentle man coming and going. Thinking: *The front of her shoes hits the ground first. He has a slight limp.*

Once, someone trod on my shoulder in the middle of a performance, but I wasn't injured. I didn't open my mouth once, other than letting out a quiet yelp. I lay there forever, recalling the director's promise. Once I successfully played the role of a corpse, he would make me the lead next time.

❊

Two months later, instead of the lead in a play, I had become a con artist. The play had bombed, pushing the troupe to the brink of bankruptcy. Desperate to save the troupe, the director launched a website—I don't know where he came up with the idea. The website promised "high-class acting, with skilled experts coming to your rescue."

Basically the director wanted to rent us out to civilians. The moment we saved enough money, he said, we would stage plays again. Nobody believed him. All the lead actors left, leaving behind the lighting director, one crew member, one supporting actor, and me. We were all thinking the same thing, even though we didn't say it out loud. We would do this job until we found something better.

Our first mission was to eat. We were to go to the director's mother's kimchi jjigae restaurant and pretend to be customers. Apparently business was slow and she was struggling.

Your mother runs a restaurant? I asked. Why haven't you brought us? Well, the director said, hesitating, she was very opposed to my choice of career. She still disapproves, even though I'm already a director.

When I went to the restaurant a few days later, it was empty, with only his mother inside. When she saw me she slowly got to her feet to take my order, then brought out kimchi jjigae from the kitchen. The jjigae was stunningly bad. There was no flavor to be discerned. I forced myself to empty an entire bowl of rice.

Before leaving, I used a pair of small tongs to help myself to a mint from the dish by the register and accidentally picked them all up. The director's mother just watched as I tried to wrench one off. It was almost winter; how long had the mints been melted together like that? I ended up leaving without one.

When I got home, Jeongsu was there. There's some pizza left, he said. Do you want some? I told him I'd already eaten and put the pizza in the freezer. He had scratched out the celebrity's face on the pizza box. It must be Taejun.

Taejun used to live in our studio apartment before he got famous. When we first toured the place, the real estate agent had talked about how it was a lucky place for aspiring actors, and we had signed papers that same day, enthralled by the word *lucky*. Now, two years in, Jeongsu had quit his ten-year pursuit of acting. And he cursed every time he saw Taejun on TV.

When he was despondent, food was the only thing that helped. He had gained a frightening amount of weight in the last six months. I couldn't even remember what he looked like in a button-down and jeans. He had been vowing he would lose weight, but he'd left only two slices of pizza in the box. I didn't say anything, though. Because we broke up six months ago.

The security deposit still loomed threateningly over us even after love withered away. We lived together, but we didn't love or even fight with each other. Should we turn off the light? Sure. Most days that was the extent of our conversation. In fact, even on the day we broke up I'd asked before bed, Should we turn off the light? Jeongsu had turned it off without answering, and we had lain silently in the dark room, close enough to touch if we reached out, until we fell asleep.

❋

These days I ate kimchi jjigae nearly every day. It still tasted like nothing, and the mints were still stuck together, but there was nothing else for me to do. All that had come in during that time were requests to make phone calls for someone else. I broke up with people on behalf of clients and called a man's parents, pretending to be his girlfriend.

The lighting director was the busiest among us. The most popular request was for a father. He even bought a new suit because he had to go to so many meetings with future in-laws, weddings, and first birthday parties. So when I got my first real referral, I wondered if I should buy a new outfit.

The client was a man in his late thirties, looking for a woman to introduce to his parents. I called the client, following the director's manual. He picked up and immediately asked if I could meet him right away. There's an additional fee for in-person consultations, I said. The client said that was fine.

Two hours later, we met up at a café near Hyehwa station. I was unsettled when I laid eyes on him, because he didn't look like he was in his late thirties; he clearly was north of fifty. He sat down and confessed that there was no meeting with the parents. He hadn't thought we would accept his case if he told the truth over the phone, so he had lied to get me here.

I started plotting my escape. We had made it clear in the ads that we would not be available for X-rated purposes, but there were always men who tried things. I started to get up, and that was when he desperately asked me to help him prepare for hibernation. Hibernation? Sleeping through winter? At that unexpected twist, I paused and studied him. And this was what he told me.

When he was young, the man held a short-term, part-time job at a cold storage facility. His job was to pack dried radish stems in ten-kilo units and move them into cold storage. Then, in the blink of an eye, the unthinkable happened. A manager who hadn't noticed him in the corner had closed the door on him.

The man figured they would open the door soon, but they didn't. He quickly lost sensation in his fingers and toes, and at some point he fell asleep. He was found two weeks later.

But then I woke up, the man said. I don't know what happened while I was asleep, but now my body is able to change according to the temperature outside. Simply put, I became a cold-blooded animal. He said this earnestly, in his pressed suit. When I didn't respond, he took out a thermometer. He put it in his ear and waited, then showed me what it said: 82.6 degrees. I wasn't moved. A thermometer could easily be tampered with. Realizing that I didn't believe him, he put the thermometer away and sat up straight again.

I'm not crazy. I worked an office job for over thirty years. All I ask is for you to bury me. Then I'll pay you ten million won. There's more if you come back at Gyeongchip and dig me out. I paused at the words *ten million won*. What does burying you entail? I asked. The man said it was literally just burying him, putting him in the ground with only his head poking out. I was horrified. You want to be buried alive?

Maybe for anyone else it would mean being buried alive, but that's not the case for me, he said. You know how frogs and snakes hibernate in the ground over winter? It's because the temperature doesn't fluctuate as much underground. But what if I forget to take you out in the spring? I scheduled a text to 119 just in case, the man said easily. I had nothing else to object to. The man said that he would find another service if I refused. So I ended up saying I would do it. Ten million! I couldn't turn that down.

The next day, the man and I were standing halfway up a mountain. Unlike my expectation that we would need to go somewhere rural, he took me to the mountains near Hongje station. Don't worry, he said as we hiked up. Nobody comes here. And hiding in broad daylight is the easiest. He told me to memorize the route. Along the way we tied colored ribbons to some of the trees. Red, then blue, then yellow. If you took about twenty steps from that tree to the left, you would get to the place he had chosen.

You can't see this place from a helicopter because of the tree canopy, he explained. He said he'd come up a few days ago and spent five hours digging. Wouldn't it be easier to go into cold storage? I asked. He said that wasn't possible because the motor was too loud. Why in the world do you want to hibernate? I asked. You know how they say things will get better after you sleep on it? I need a long time to sleep on it, the man said calmly.

Then he went into the hole. I moved the dirt back on top of him. Shoveling the dirt was easier than I'd thought it would be, but it was still strange, because it felt as though I were burying him alive. It was fairly terrifying to see only his head poking out aboveground.

I put up a small pup tent around his head. Inside, we had one last conversation. He told me to open an inner pocket in the tent. I found a ten-million-won check. Okay, see you next year at Gyeongchip, he said. Maybe the dirt on top of him was heavy, because he sort of struggled to speak. Good luck, I said, and left the tent.

I walked back down the hill and didn't see a single person. As I headed over to the subway station, I couldn't believe all this had happened in broad daylight.

❊

He must have frozen to death by now, was my first thought upon waking. I didn't believe any of that stuff about being a cold-blooded animal or that his body temperature was 82.6 degrees. This man was attempting suicide in a novel way, and I had been paid ten million won to help him.

I lay next to sleeping Jeongsu for another hour, then quietly brushed my teeth, just as quietly changed, and left. Subway, then bus, then red ribbon, blue ribbon, yellow ribbon, twenty paces to the left. Then I opened the zipper of the tent.

Who is it? shouted the man, startled. Me, the person who buried you yesterday, I said, stuffing myself into the tent. I just don't think this is right. If you die like this, that means I've committed murder. I was hibernating, the man said. What do you mean, hibernating? I raised my voice. If you don't believe me, why did you willingly bury me yesterday? he demanded. I made the wrong decision for ten million won, I said. I've finally come to my senses. I can't leave you to die like this. I grabbed the shovel in the corner. I'm going to have to dig you out.

Please stop, the man said. Do you know how much I've done to prepare for this moment? I ignored him and began to dig. The man shouted, Please don't, stop, and so on, but I didn't stop. When I uncovered his shoulders, he shouted at me in a low voice, Listen to me, you fucking bitch.

Bury me, he said. I told you, bury me. I stopped. I was about to bury him again, but my hands were shaking so much that I kept fumbling. Eventually, when he was buried up to his chin again, the man relaxed and closed his eyes. Please leave now, the man said politely, using honorifics again. I managed to calm my pounding heart as I put the shovel down and left the tent. Then I took in deep breath after deep breath. You couldn't see this spot even from a helicopter. A spot in the middle of Seoul where nobody could hear you scream. It was just me and this guy here.

Stores came into view as I got down the mountain, and my terror slowly subsided. Shame crashed over me, leaving behind anger. But this was an emotional change I'd already experienced several times. Every time it hit me, I felt helpless, but in the end I moved past it. I figured my anger would fizzle out.

And that was why I was a little out of sorts. Whether I was eating or sleeping, what happened that day kept popping into my head. Even after a few days, the way the man's mouth moved as he said *you fucking bitch* and the way my shovel kept missing the mark remained vivid in my mind. One night, in the early-morning hours, I remembered how I cried as I shoveled dirt back on the man, and I couldn't stand it anymore. I shook Jeongsu awake.

Come with me to the mountains, I said. The mountains? Jeongsu said, still half in dreamland. I spoke directly in his ear: Someone's buried there. Who? Someone who cursed me out. Jeongsu's eyes flew open. Did you kill someone? No, he's sleeping there. I explained everything to him. How I had been renting out my acting skills, how I had buried the man, and how I now wanted my revenge, all of it.

I'm confused, Jugyeong, he said, sitting up. Didn't we break up? Yeah, I said. So what is all this? I just looked at Jeongsu, who was five eight and was tilting past 220 pounds. I'll give you a hundred thousand won if you go with me, I offered. That seemed like the appropriate rate.

So is this guy a hippie? Jeongsu asked before we started up the hill. I told him it wasn't like that. He says he wants to hibernate in the mountains. That's why he's buried underground. Jeongsu stared at me and asked me what I was talking about. So . . . imagine a pot of kimjang kimchi, I said, then told him to stop asking questions.

I told Jeongsu to hush when we spotted the tree with the red ribbon on it. We walked gingerly so we wouldn't make a ruckus stepping on the leaves. The man didn't wake up even when we opened the tent. Jeongsu was horrified to see the man buried up to his neck. What if he's already dead? he whispered in my ear.

I dragged him into the tent. It was snug in there, so we sat across from each other with the man's head between us. We craned down to look into his face, and we both turned quiet. He looked entirely at ease. Like the face of a newborn baby, without a wisp of sadness. I cautiously placed a finger under his nose. After maybe thirty seconds, a slow, warm puff reached my hand. He really must be hibernating, I marveled. He's breathing super slow. Jeongsu put his hand there, too, and looked shocked.

Now what? he asked. Let's wake him up, I said. Jeongsu yelled into the man's ear, and the man screamed and woke up. He swiveled his head around and was shocked to see us. What happened? It's not Gyeongchip yet, the man said, his voice cracking.

You were terrible to Jugyeong, said Jeongsu. Who's Jugyeong? the man asked. Me, I said. Don't you remember what happened? The man scowled. I don't know what you're talking about. I have to sleep. It can be really dangerous if I keep waking up. You can go to sleep after you apologize, I said, and the man let out a deep sigh. His breath stank. The man looked not at me but at Jeongsu and said, I'm sorry, now please leave. I couldn't help myself. I spat in his face.

Before we went to sleep that night, I asked Jeongsu, Why did *you* spit in his face? Because you did, he replied. There must have been a reason for it. That was what I'd told him when we broke up.

When Jeongsu said we should break up, I'd said, Okay. Is that it? Jeongsu had asked, and I had said, There must have been a reason for it. I didn't realize he would remember what I'd said.

Don't tell anyone what happened today, I said, changing the subject. I won't, he said. And then we lay on our backs, side by side, and stared up at the ceiling. Jeongsu fell asleep first.

❊

Perhaps the director had done some marketing, because our business took off. Requests for phone calls kept coming in, and I was assigned in-person jobs a few times a week. I took on the role of a friend, a girlfriend, and even an undercover investigator of sorts. I shrieked that I found an errant hair in my coffee or made a big to-do out of nothing in order to report the rude staff at the government office.

All of that had stemmed from a client asking for help tanking the business of a rival café and another client who had been so jealous of a friend who had passed the ninth-level civil service exam that I was hired to harass that friend. I filed a report on the government portal that accepted complaints and kept calling the government office to lodge my displeasure. I received my payment when that civil servant was disciplined.

All the clients have something in common, I told the director. The director was trying to upgrade the job bulletin board on our website. Everyone is trying to protect themselves by harming other people. Jugyeong, that's what everyone does, the director said, his eyes glued to the screen. He was right. That triggered so many questions: Why did lies edge closer to the truth the more you lied? Did the director also start having nightmares? Did the director actually want to put on plays again?

Director, I said, and he finally turned to look at me. What? he asked. What is it? After a while I asked, Are the mints at your mother's restaurant for customers? The director smiled with embarrassment. Don't touch those. They've been there since she opened the place.

I got on the bus to go home. I took a seat and checked my phone, only to find a text from Jeongsu: *Coming home late?* I texted back to say I was on my way. Maybe it was strange, but we were being nicer to each other after going up the mountain together. We checked to see when the other person was coming home, and the person getting ready for bed first unfolded the bedding for the other person. We had stopped doing such things when we broke up. All we'd done was go up a mountain and spit in a man's face, but weirdly I felt closer to Jeongsu.

But Jeongsu still didn't know that I had ten million won. Even in the middle of washing my face I would come out of the bathroom to stare at the seven zeros stamped in my bankbook. With ten million in my pocket, I could immediately leave both the director and Jeongsu. That reality actually made me stay.

Back home, Jeongsu was waiting for me with omurice, ketchup fried rice topped with a thin omelet that you could cut into with a spoon. It had been my favorite when we were together. What made you cook? I asked. Just because, he said. We silently tucked in. Halfway through the meal, Jeongsu said, That hibernating guy—are you going to go see him again? No, I said, but I changed my mind once I swallowed the food in my mouth. Well, I guess I might.

What for? he asked. He said he'd pay me more if I woke him up at Gyeongchip, I said. So he's just stuck there if you don't? he asked. No, he scheduled a text to 119 the day after Gyeongchip, I explained. Hey, this omurice is so good. I ate up all of Jeongsu's leftovers, too.

Jeongsu said he'd do the dishes, too. I didn't insist. Instead I played the IU concert he liked on YouTube for him, but an ad popped up before the end of the first song; it was Taejun's beverage ad. The mood turned grim for about five minutes, but Jeongsu didn't show much of a reaction.

As soon as he finished the dishes, he asked again: Are you really going to go see him? I said I was thinking about it. Why do you keep asking? You want to come with me? I said that as a joke, but Jeongsu took it seriously and said he would. I'll go with you, he said. It could get dangerous. Okay, I said breezily, but the moment he said *dangerous*, I remembered how the man had cursed at me.

So I wrapped my blanket around myself after I got ready for bed and asked, Guess what I am? This was a game we played a lot in the troupe. One person physically mimed what they were thinking of, and the rest of the group had to guess what it was. Gimbap? Nope. Blood sausage? Nope. A log of poop? Are you serious? What is it? The hibernating guy. Jeongsu laughed a little, and only then did I feel a little less worried.

❊

I'm so jealous, I said to the lighting director as he gave me a travel mug with a snowflake emblazoned on it. He had received it as a party favor at the first-birthday party he went to yesterday. Ever since he started this gig he was eating at buffets practically daily and receiving expensive gift bags. Who knew that being a father would be so useful? Earlier in the morning, I had washed and dried my face with the soap and towel the lighting director had brought back from a wedding.

It pissed me off. I grumbled to the director as he dozed in a chair: Why do you only give me such awful roles? Last week I had to spill coffee on someone going to an interview. *He* gets to stuff himself at buffets, and I just get cursed out. Okay, the director said, how about I get you a gig as a wedding guest next week? That wasn't what I wanted, though. I didn't want a role in which I applauded for someone; I wanted a role in which *I* would be applauded. But I gave up and said my goodbyes.

Today's destination was a café. A customer's dog had snuck out and gone missing when the owner propped the door open to clean. Can you just tell her that you opened the door? asked the owner on the phone. Just tell her you left it open as you were leaving. I'll go out of business if people find out it was my mistake. I said I would. This was nothing compared to what I'd been doing.

When I got to the café, the client was sitting at a table with the owner of the dog, a woman in her late thirties who didn't bother saying hello. I apologized as soon as I sat down. The café owner explained, Our regular here made a mistake. She's come all this way to apologize in person. I hope you'll be able to forgive her.

The woman didn't answer. I raised my head to peek at her. She was looking out the window. I glanced at the client. She shot a look at the dog owner and shrugged. I'm so very sorry, I said again. She still didn't react. Ten minutes passed like that.

Uhp, uhp. The woman began making a weird noise with her mouth closed. *Uhp, uhp, uhp.* It was a moan, a strangled sound, and she kept it up. The client and I looked at each other, startled. She made that noise for a while, then said, Before he came to live with me, Potato had vocal cord surgery, so that's the only sound he can make even when he's scared out of his mind. Silence stretched over us again. From far away we could hear a car honking, someone calling someone else. Suddenly the woman said, You can go.

Before heading home I stopped by the convenience store and bought four imported beers that Jeongsu liked. Jeongsu was thrilled, saying he had been in the mood for beer. We drank them while snacking on shrimp chips. The electric floor mat was so warm; I lay on top of it. He lay down, too. You know that guy? I said. I'm going to go wake him up in the spring. The hibernating guy? Yeah, I said. You spat in his face; you think he'll pay you? he asked. It's not because of the money, I explained. I feel like I'm going to keep worrying about him if I don't. I raised myself up to take a sip of beer and lay back down. Okay, then let's go together, Jeongsu said.

My frozen body felt warm on the heated floor. Hey, Jeongsu, I said. Yeah. Guess what this is. I covered my mouth with a hand and made a sound, *uhp, uhp*. A dog? Nope. A mouse? Nope. A hostage? Nope. What is it? I didn't tell him.

❊

I told the director that I was taking the week off. He asked what was going on. Nothing, I said. Jugyeong, you know I don't give you bad roles on purpose, he said. I know, I said before hanging up.

Three days into my week of rest, Jeongsu asked, Did you quit your job? No, I said. Then why are you home? he asked. It's winter break, I said. Jeongsu didn't respond and headed to his part-time job. But I wasn't joking. As a child it had terrified me that adults didn't have winter break. That was why I'd decided to give myself one.

Lying down, I listened to instrumental music until I got hungry, then made myself curry. I liked the process of making curry better than eating it. I liked simmering hard vegetables for a long time until they turned soft, warming the cold room in the process. I ate in the quiet.

A long time ago, I'd peeked in Jeongsu's diary. It wasn't too long after we'd started living together. *Jugyeong talks in her sleep sometimes. When I hear that—* That was where the entry stopped. For a long time I wondered what was supposed to follow. Sometimes I thought of great endings: *it makes me love her more, it makes me pull the blanket over her, I think I'm going to have nice dreams*. Sometimes I thought of awful endings: *it makes me hate her, it makes me feel suffocated, it makes me want to die*. At one point I could spend all night awake thinking about the possibilities. I ate all the curry without leaving even a tiny bit.

On the sixth day of my winter break, I washed the dishes and mopped the floor, whistling. At some point Jeongsu had told me that if I whistled for as long as I could whenever I had bad thoughts, I would forget all about them.

I kept whistling, then decided to go out. I put my shoes on for the first time in six days. But once I left the apartment I couldn't think of where to go. I agonized over all the choices but ended up at the kimchi jjigae restaurant.

As soon as she saw me, the director's mother said, I was hoping you'd be back. She said I'd left something behind last time. She reached under the counter and brought out a hairpin, a sparkly red ribbon, and placed it in my palm. I told her thank you and slid it in my hair. It looks so good on you, she said.

The kimchi jjigae was still terrible. It was comforting to think that her kimchi jjigae would be bad next year and ten years into the future. I ate an entire bowl of rice with the jjigae, and she handed me a tangerine for dessert. I left the peel, star-like, on the table.

When I got home, Jeongsu asked what I had in my hair. A hairpin, of course, I said. You hate that stuff, he said. I told him I decided to like them. But when I went to the bathroom and looked in the mirror, all I could see was the pin. I yanked it out and was about to toss it, but the trash can was full. I stepped out of the bathroom and said, Let's have a whistling contest. Loser takes the garbage out. What's a whistling contest? he asked. Seeing who can whistle the longest. Wasn't it your turn to throw out the garbage this week? he asked. No, I said.

But then I lost. I had no idea he could whistle for so long. I grabbed the two trash bags and went outside. I borrowed Jeongsu's puffer coat, which was big and warm. My hands were freezing, so on the way back in I shoved them in the pockets. A bunch of crumpled receipts were wadded inside. He always shoved trash in his pockets and never cleared them out. I was always forced to check the pockets before doing laundry.

I took out the receipts. *Sundaeguk 6,500 won. Bacchus 800 won. Samgak gimbap 1,200 won.* The last receipt was from two weeks ago. Then I spotted a coupon among the receipts. It was a frequent customer coupon for a café named Dajeong, marked with eight stamps. Was he seeing someone?

I stopped in front of our door and stared down at the coupon. Eight smiley-face stamps. Two more beverages and he could get a free drink of his choice. On the bottom was the café's address and phone number in small print; the address seemed familiar. Where was that? As I stood there thinking, the sensor light above me turned off.

Why did you go see him? I asked as I flung open the door. Jeongsu was lying down, on his phone; he looked up at me. It had come to me in front of our door, in the dark. That café was near the mountain where I'd buried the hibernating guy, where you had to take the subway and then the bus and then had to keep going.

I'm asking because I just don't get it, I said. Why did you go there? He didn't answer, so I asked again. Did you go alone? He said he had. What did you do there? I woke him up, he said. You went all the way there just to wake him up? I demanded. Jeongsu didn't speak for a long time. Because it's so unfair, he finally said. When he continued, his voice was low and calm: We have to freeze and get sick and make rent and pay for the heat and buy winter clothes and work all winter long, and that guy's just sleeping. What else could I do? All I can think about at work is that guy's face. I can't stand it.

Isn't that why you spat in his face? Jeongsu asked in the same disdainful tone he employed when criticizing Taejun's acting. After a long silence I spoke: He'll die if he can't sleep and keeps getting woken up. No, Jeongsu said. Every time I wake him up I give him something to drink. I remembered the eight stamps on the coupon. I thought of Jeongsu taking the subway to the bus and walking up the mountain to wake the guy up. Pouring a beverage down the throat of a guy who only had his head sticking out of the ground and doing that eight separate times.

I stalked into the apartment without bothering to take off my shoes and began packing. What are you doing? Jeongsu asked, but I didn't answer. I grabbed my toiletries and a few extra sets of clothes and left. Jeongsu didn't try to stop me or follow me out.

I took a cab to the theater. In my bag I had the spare key the director had given me. I sent a text to 119 in the cab and turned off my phone. It was late at night, without a speck of snow falling. I looked out the window and all I saw were bare tree and pale lamppost, bare tree and pale lamppost, bare tree and pale lamppost.

The cabbie said it was going to be hard to drive into the alley with all the cars parked illegally. I got out and walked. When I was six, the woman who lived across from us had fallen asleep in the car with the heater on and died. All throughout my childhood I was petrified of finding a dead body at night, inside a parked car.

I opened the door and went down to the basement, into the theater. The theater was so dark that I couldn't see my hand in front of my face. The director used that to his benefit, making the demonic woman appear in the audience the moment the lights turned on again. Everyone would scream, and even though I knew it was coming, it startled me every time.

With the theater lights on, I lay in the corner of the stage, using my scarf as a pillow. Something poked me in my pocket, and when I took it out I realized it was the hairpin. I slid it back in my hair and wondered, Who was the owner of the pin? Was she my age? How long was her hair? I got scared again, and I wished that anyone, even if it was that demonic woman, would come in and sit on my belly. And drink a glass of gin.

Even Though It's Not Alaska

1. A thin white straw

Last night I dreamt of Alaska. I kept my eyes closed for a while to hold on to the sparkling glaciers and the beautiful aurora. I hung out in bed for a long time before finally getting up to open the curtains, but something pierced the sole of my foot. With a shriek I collapsed on the floor. I looked at my foot: there was a small drop of blood.

I searched the floor and saw something tiny poking up. It was so small that I couldn't grab it with my fingers. With tweezers I yanked it out, and, shockingly, what emerged was a straw. A thin white straw used for drinking yogurt. On closer examination two straws had been taped end to end, making it very long. Why was a straw stuck in my floor? And two of them at that? I held the long straw in my hand, confounded, but first decided to bandage my foot.

❄

For four years I worked as a bookkeeper at a small company until I was let go at the beginning of the year. The CEO said I wasn't a team player. He told me I should try going to lunch with my coworkers at my next job. What a load of crap. There was no reason for me to eat with my coworkers at my new job. Because a month ago, I had become an assassin.

I became an assassin solely to get my revenge. I used to have two incredibly important creatures in my life. They were stray tabby brothers named Seongcheol and Byeongcheol. They were my only friends, my only family. Every day for three years I had prepared food for them, until a month ago, when two stray dogs showed up and snatched them in front of my eyes. The following day I combed the mountain in my neighborhood until I came across Seongcheol's body, but I never did find Byeongcheol.

Everything changed after I started dreaming of revenge. I was no longer a layabout but an assassin; my daily planner turned into a detailed blueprint; and my studio on the edge of Seoul became a secret base. My main staple became the dried pollock I'd bought in bulk for Seongcheol and Byeongcheol. Every morning I gulped down hot bugeo guk, plotting revenge.

I was washing the dishes when the doorbell rang. Who is it? I called, and the person said she was from downstairs. I opened the door and found a woman wearing shorts, although it was the middle of winter. Did you happen to see a straw? she asked. Are you talking about a thin white straw? I asked. Yes, yes, that's right. Where did you find it? she asked. It was stuck in my floor, I said. She said she thought that would be the case and asked if she could come in and check my floor. Taken aback, I told her she could.

She crouched on my floor and looked at the tiny pinprick of a hole. She felt it with her hand and took a few pictures with her phone. How did you know there was a straw? I asked. Because I made the hole, she said, and I'm the one who put the straw in it. Stunned, I stared at her. Why would you do that? I asked. Well, it's a long story, she said.

We sat at my kitchen table, facing each other. Everything started with dust, she explained. One day, she was lying in bed when a strange white dust fell on her face. She looked closely and saw a tiny nick in her ceiling, and the dust seemed to be falling from there. *Do we have pests, or is the building constructed shoddily?* she wondered, but she moved on without giving it much thought. But dust kept falling on her the next day and the day after that. As she brushed the dust off her face, she realized something. This powdery dust didn't fall when she wasn't in bed. Only when she was in bed, staring at the ceiling, did dust rain down from the hole.

Now you understand, right? she asked me suddenly. Understand what? I asked. I stared at the ceiling so hard that I bore a hole through it, she said, and explained that she had tried to stick a pen in the hole to see how big it was, but it didn't fit. Neither did a chopstick nor a cotton swab. But when she stuck a thin white straw in, it had slid right in until it got stuck. From then on, she pushed the straw in deeper whenever she thought of it. She was clearly boring through the ceiling with her gaze, and it had taken three whole months for two straws to come up through my floor.

She's insane, but she has such beautiful fingers, I thought as I watched her. As she spoke she stroked the cup of coffee I'd given her, and when she did the jellyfish tattoo on her left pointer and middle fingers undulated as though swimming. She said she would compensate me for the hole in my floor. It's fine, I said. Just don't keep sticking straws up there. She kept insisting she would pay me, and after some back and forth she gave me her business card. Come on down if you ever want a tattoo, she said, it's on the house. I looked down at the black card that said *Tattoo Artist*. Her name was Yu.

2. I am a cat

After Yu left, I drank my cooled coffee and studied the floor. It was a tiny speck of a hole, but thirty centimeters deep. What did she use to make the hole? I wondered, placing my finger on it. I didn't want all the secrets and hostility that filled my place to leak out.

My life turned simple once I'd become an assassin. I had bugeo guk every morning, then practiced sprinting and shooting in the empty lot, and from time to time I ventured into the mountains where stray dogs lived. The most important was sprinting. It was critical to run fast to catch the dogs. When I ran, there came a moment when blisters formed on the soles of my feet and my lungs felt ready to burst. But each time I reminded myself: *I am a cat.*

I wasn't joking. Nobody knew this, but I actually *was* a cat. Seongcheol and Byeongcheol were the ones to inform me of that truth. Once, I'd found myself on the verge of tears as I prepared their food. Work had been particularly rough that day. My coworkers ignored me, I felt unwelcome during lunch, and my boss's abusive language was getting harder to brush off.

I was about to head back home when Seongcheol and Byeongcheol blocked my way. I tried to shoo them away, but they didn't move; they meowed at me. Strangely, that day I could understand what they were saying. The cats said, *Suyeong, things are hard for you because you're a cat, not a human. Look, look, see how you can understand us? You know what it's like to not fit in, to be on the margins; you know what it's like to lead a life where you're fleeing dozens if not hundreds of times a day.*

The tight ball in my chest dissolved instantly; everything now made perfect sense. *It's because I am a cat that I don't fit in with people at work,* I realized. Everything changed once I discovered the truth. Beginning the next day, I didn't laugh at my boss's unpleasant jokes and just ate by myself at lunch. I keyed the car of a coworker who'd started a rumor that I was crazy. I realized for the first time why cats needed sharp claws. I was completely alone, but that didn't bum me out like it had before. It was a given for me to be abused, to be lonely. After all, I was the only cat among these horrible humans. Once I accepted that truth, I felt more at ease than ever before.

That had been the first and only time I understood what Seongcheol and Byeongcheol were saying, but no matter. Cats understood one another even without speaking. Those two were the only creatures in the entire world who understood me. How could I forgive the dogs that took them away?

Last month I'd installed a trap in the hills, but the dogs didn't fall for it. So now I would have to capture them with my bare hands. I opened my backpack, where I kept the tranquilizer gun I'd bought with my severance pay. Seongcheol was dead, but Byeongcheol could still be alive. I would capture the dogs and find out what happened to Byeongcheol. Once I got the answer, I would do to them exactly what they had done to Seongcheol and Byeongcheol.

Once I got my revenge, I would leave for Alaska, where there were more glaciers than traffic lights, where permafrost glinted. I wanted to live out the rest of my days there, not as a human or as a cat, but as ice. Ice doesn't think, ice doesn't need anything. I liked that. I'd already turned into a cat, so why wouldn't I be able to turn into ice?

3. The hole and a secret

A few days later, I looked down at the hole and noticed it had gotten wider. Now a regular straw would fit, not just the skinny white one. I headed straight downstairs. The hole is getting wider, I blurted out when Yu opened the door.

Come on in, Yu said, I work out of my apartment. Her place was messy, with tattoo sketches pasted all over the walls, and when she pulled a black curtain to the side I saw a twin bed back there. She stepped on the bed and looked up. You're right, it's definitely gotten bigger. I'll try sleeping with my head by the foot of the bed.

Do you really think you made it by staring at it? Shouldn't we try to figure out if something else made it? I asked carefully. Yu said firmly that there was no need: I know I bored into it. She looked so confident that I found myself nodding. Then I noticed a long tattoo on her wrist. Is that a straw? I asked, and Yu said it was. It's something worth commemorating, she said. *Unbelievable, she's commemorated boring a hole through someone else's floor,* I thought. Yu was already moving her pillow to the foot of the bed. I watched her do that, then went back home feeling uneasy.

Then came another unexpected problem. When I lay down to sleep at night, I kept hearing weird noises—*ughhhh, eeek*. At first I thought it was a ghost and got scared, but when I listened more closely I realized it was coming from downstairs. Her clients must be groaning in pain as they got their tattoos, the sound traveling up through the hole. Finally, one morning when the dark circles under my eyes had stretched down to my chin, I put on my coat.

A long time after I rang her bell, Yu finally came out, her face puffy. If you were sleeping I can come back later, I said.

No, it's okay. What's going on? she asked. It's the noise, I told her. People are making weird sounds at night and I can hear them through the hole. Yu said it hadn't occurred to her that it might be too loud and said she would be more careful. I nodded, then said what I had been rehearsing to myself. I'd like to get a tattoo; when would be a good time? Yu rubbed sleep out of her eyes. Now's good.

To be honest, I had been wanting to get a small glacier on my left wrist the moment she'd offered to give me one. I would think of Alaska every time I looked at it. Nobody knew what was buried in the Alaskan glaciers. Corpses, maybe, or shipwrecks, or an enormous forest. The glaciers were thousands of years old, frozen solid, burying all secrets. I wanted to freeze, too, with Seongcheol and Byeongcheol buried in my heart. Yu swiftly drew a glacier on a sheet of transfer paper, and when she applied it to my wrist, an ink outline of a glacier remained on my skin. We chatted as we waited for the ink to dry. It turned out we were the same age, so we agreed to stop using honorifics. Who's this? I asked about a picture on her desk. A man who kind of looked like her was grinning in the photo. My boyfriend, she said, but he has another girlfriend.

When Yu told her boyfriend she liked him, he let her know that he already had a girlfriend. But you kept seeing him? I asked. Because I didn't want to lose him, she said, matter-of-factly, so I concealed my shock. Yu said she hadn't told anyone about this, that she could tell me these things because I knew about the hole.

We didn't speak while she worked on me. The pain wasn't too bad, and twenty minutes later I had a glacier on my wrist. I instantly fell in love with it. I thanked her and was about to leave, but Yu asked me to wait and put on her coat. I'm going for a smoke on the third floor, she said. Come with me. I don't smoke, I said. Then just come hang out, she said.

So I went down to the third floor with her, where there was an outdoor walkway that connected our building to the adjacent one. We leaned against the railing and looked out. Bare trees lined the sidewalk, and cars drove by sparingly on the four-lane road in front. I love winter. The season that creates more space in the streets, more space on the trees. I felt lighter in the cold air and let out a big breath. My breath and Yu's cigarette smoke drifted away in similar shapes.

You didn't expect that about my boyfriend, did you? Yu asked suddenly. Not really, I said. I know it's bad, she said, looking down at the road. That's why I don't tell anyone.

Unfortunately for Yu, I didn't understand people. Why did people sign up for sorrow? The world was already filled with sadness.

Do you believe me when I say that I made the hole by staring at it? Yu asked, and I said I wasn't sure. Maybe she did make the hole. Some things were inexplicable, like how I turned out to be a cat. Yu finished her cigarette, but we stood there quietly, looking out, until we got bored.

I don't know what Yu did, but I didn't hear anything that night. I was so unaccustomed to the sudden quiet that I got back up from bed. I went to the bathroom and took my two softest towels, rolled them up, and started to pet them. I knew, of course, that I was petting towels, and that towels had no deep significance other than comfort, but I still did it. That night, hugging two rolled towels to my chest, I wondered why it was so easy to love and yet so hard, until I fell asleep.

4. Nothing had happened by the water this summer

Today, my morning bugeo guk was perfectly seasoned, I shaved a few seconds off my time in my sprint session, and shooting practice was a success. I was ready. Now, all I had to do was pick the date of vengeance. As soon as I was done, I would terminate my lease, take my security deposit, and head to Alaska.

On my way home I got a text. I figured it would be spam, but it was actually Yu. Without any explanation she just told me to come to the underground parking garage. I went down and heard her call out, Over here. I went toward her voice and found her standing next to a black Chevy Malibu. She said she bought it as a birthday present for herself; her birthday was next week. Let's go for a drive, she said. It's used but in great condition.

What wasn't great was Yu's driving. Horns blared as soon as she merged onto the street. It turned out that she hadn't driven since she got her license years ago. I didn't dare let go of the passenger-side handle the entire time she drove, but she herself was relaxed, even leisurely tapping the steering wheel with a finger when we were at a red light. I noticed the jellyfish tattoo I'd first seen when I met her, swimming gently along her fingers. Did they have jellyfish in Alaska? I wondered, then shook my head.

Twenty minutes in, I asked, Where are we going? I don't know, she said. We glanced at each other. She drove terribly and the heater of this used car blew out a stench like rotten cheese, but I was in a good mood. The city nightscape was incredibly beautiful, the December streets twinkling with bright Christmas decorations. I felt sorry for the trees wrapped in glowing hot bulbs, but they were gorgeous. After driving around for a while, she remembered a lakeside café she'd gone to with her boyfriend.

When we finally got to the café, a sign on the door said *Thank you for your support over the years*. We stared at it, then decided to walk along the lake. As we did, Yu told me about the last time she'd come here. It was monsoon season, so the water level was higher. Yu and her boyfriend had spent a nice time together, joking around with each other as they walked along the lake, but she was suddenly gripped by an urge to push him in. She balled her fists so she wouldn't, clenching her hands so hard that her nails had dug into her palms, nicking them. Isn't that crazy? Yu asked.

We stopped and gazed at the lake shrouded in darkness. I don't think that's crazy, I said. *Anyone could imagine killing someone,* I thought. They said that thirty bottles of Chilsung cider were sold every minute in Korea. I could guarantee that even more people were dying in someone's imagination every minute, every second. That really wasn't remarkable. Nothing had happened by the water this past summer. But I was different. I wouldn't just imagine it. I would really capture and kill them.

A while ago my boyfriend suggested I get another boyfriend, Yu said. You should, I said earnestly. Instead of responding, Yu snapped off a reed and tossed it in the water. Then something unexpected: fish mistook it for food and swam over. Small mouths opened and closed above the dark surface of the water. It was a weirdly depressing sight. *Damn it, they are so desperate, and damn it, it's so cold.* We shoved our hands in our pockets and hurried back to the car. Snow fell on our way back, and by the time we got home it had thickened into a snowstorm. It was a miracle that we got home safely.

5. Happy birthday, but . . .

The next time I saw Yu, it was a week later. Because of the huge snowstorm, my plans were on hold as I waited for the snow to melt. I didn't think it would be all that easy to chase after dogs on a snow-covered mountain. As I waited, Yu's birthday came around. She invited me over, and I didn't decline this time, either.

I went to her place with a cake and saw she had a Christmas tree. She said her boyfriend had given it to her. It's pretty, I said, looking up at it. Liar, she said, looking up at it with me.

I *was* lying, so I didn't say anything else. The tree was too big and crude in her small space. He got it online, so he didn't know it was going to be this big, Yu said, and told me she was going to throw it out right after Christmas.

We took the cake out and sat at the table. Yu closed her eyes and made a wish before blowing out the candles, and even though she didn't tell me, I could guess what she wished for. I handed her a birthday present. What's this? A voodoo doll, I said. I got one for myself, too. I took another one out of my bag and showed her. What kind of present is this? Yu grumbled, but read the directions carefully. "First," the directions stated, "stab the doll with a needle while thinking about the person you want to curse. Second, discard the cursed doll far away from home." There's no needle, though, Yu said. All you have here are needles, I reminded her.

We stabbed the dolls with tattoo needles as I thought of the two stray dogs and Yu thought of her boyfriend's girlfriend. Did you see how much it snowed a few days ago? she asked as she stabbed her doll. It was like the world was going to end. She said all her clients had canceled because of the storm. Do you think the world is really going to end? I asked, stabbing my doll. Of course, she said. When? I asked. Soon, she said. The way she was talking, it felt like the world would end tomorrow. Would I be able to see Seongcheol and Byeongcheol again if the world came to an end? I wondered, and then remembered that it snowed six meters at a time in Alaska. After I learned that factoid I had been hoping it would snow six meters in Korea at some point, too.

If six meters of snow piled up, everything would screech to a stop . . . and Seoul, always bustling, would grind to a halt, too. When I lost Seongcheol and Byeongcheol I couldn't understand how the world kept revolving as though nothing had happened. Back then, I was heartbroken with dawn's first light, and my heart broke again by sundown. If the world could halt just until six meters of snow melted, I might be able to find forgiveness in my heart. I stabbed the doll over and over again, ruminating on these idle thoughts. Was it true that hatred poisoned you? I felt lighter than ever, stabbing my doll until it was nearly in tatters.

Afterward I laid my head on the table, but Yu told me to put my coat on. Why? I asked. We have to throw the dolls away, she said. Now? Of course, she said. Are you going to be able to sleep in the same room as this thing? I looked down at the doll in my hand and put my coat on without a fuss.

We decided to throw them out as far away as possible. The problem, as always, was Yu's driving. She failed to change lanes in time, so we ended up on the highway. If you keep going it says we'll get to Busan, I said as I read the signs. Yu said we didn't need to go that far.

Well, anyway, it's nice to be on the highway in the middle of the night, I thought as we barreled down the empty road. Yu turned on songs from the nineties and the early aughts. Byun Jin Sub, Kim Hyun Chul, Yada, even Flower.

I thought it was a random selection of songs, but I enjoyed myself as I listened. Though Yu wasn't a cat, I found myself at ease when I was with her. Why are you looking at me like that? she asked after a moment, and I said, No reason.

We kept going until we got to Seoul Mannamui Gwangjang Service Area. This was where we would throw away the dolls. We tossed them into a round trash can and, deciding that it was a letdown to go home right away, bought eomuk at one of the food stands. Do you think it's going to work? Yu asked as she ate. I guess we'll find out, I said. For some reason we felt like we were waiting for something to happen, like we were coconspirators of some crime, and each gulped down two orders of eomuk, rubbing our arms against the cold.

Yu said she would stop by the bathroom. I wondered if I should wait in the car, but changed my mind and went for a short walk. It was late so there weren't that many people around. What if we kept driving into the night, like people without a plan in road trip movies? I was heading toward the back of the rest area when I stopped short. Two familiar eyes glinted in the dark under a parked car. I knew those eyes.

Seongcheol! I ran to the car and dropped to the ground. The cat, looking into my eyes, was definitely my dead Seongcheol. Seongcheol, Seongcheol, I kept calling. He didn't come out even though he saw me. Panicked, I told him I was going to get revenge on the dogs. I swear, I'm going to get revenge for you. I'm going to do it when the snow melts. That was when Seongcheol spoke: *The snow melt-*

ed three days ago. His voice was small and faint, and I could barely hear it even when I strained. I couldn't say anything to that. I'll explain everything, I begged on my knees. Come out and let's talk, Seongcheol. Show me your face, just once. But Seongcheol didn't speak again. I looked under the car with the flashlight on my phone, but there was nothing there.

I wasn't sure how long I was on the ground. Yu showed up. Did you get hurt? she shouted when she saw me. No, I said. I was looking all over for you, she said. Why aren't you answering your phone? She held out a hand to help me up. Even in the dark I could tell that the tip of Yu's nose was cherry red from the cold. Sorry, I said. Did you get lost? she asked. Yeah, I lied.

On our way home, Yu made conversation, but I didn't engage, only giving curt answers. She soon shut up, her feelings probably hurt. I felt bad, but my head was swimming with thoughts of only Seongcheol. He knew why I was feeling so terrible. At some point I stopped pushing for revenge because of the snow, because my ankle was aching—I was making up excuses. I was letting him down without even realizing it. Me, of all people, letting Seongcheol down.

6. Alaska

Stray dogs are active early in the morning when there aren't a lot of people around. I woke up at four, dressed in layers, cinched my sneakers tight. I started implementing my plan the day after I saw Seongcheol at the rest area. Today was the seventh day in a row I climbed the mountain.

The mountain at dawn was dark, steep, slippery. I was used to it now, after having fallen several times. Midway up, I set a tin of mackerel on the ground and hid behind a tree. Now it was only a matter of time. I would wait like this until a stray dog appeared within range, and I would shoot it with my tranquilizer gun. As the chill of the earth snaked slowly up my body, I gritted my teeth so they wouldn't chatter and give me away.

Even so, as I waited for dogs that didn't show up, Yu, her face, and her incomprehensible sorrow popped into my head. I had been ignoring her the last few days in order to focus on my mission. She even rang my doorbell last night, but I pretended I wasn't home. I looked down at the glacier on my wrist every time I wanted to pick up her call or open the door for her so my heart would freeze solid again. So that I would stop thinking.

I was trying to push all that out of my mind when I heard faint rustling from far away. I held my breath and glared at the direction of the noise. In the dim light, I could see an animal coming closer. Finally, after a week, a stray dog had shown up. The dog went up to the tin, looked around, and started slobbering up the fish. My blood boiled as I watched. A brown tail on a white body. It was one of the dogs that had attacked Seongcheol and Byeongcheol.

Certain that this was it, I aimed calmly at the dog. I had to hit it square on the back leg. It might die if I accidentally shot it in the heart or the head. But thankfully, at close range, the tranq hit my target. Startled, the dog turned and started sprinting back to where it had come from. I set my teeth and dashed after it. A dog could run for five to ten minutes after being hit by a tranq dart. I had run hundreds, thousands of times around a vacant lot for this very moment. The dog ran deeper into steeper terrain to get away from me. The cold wind cut my ears. Branches scratched my arms and face. I didn't care. I ran.

I lost sight of the dog but searched maniacally until I found it collapsed in a pile of leaves. I slung it over my shoulder. I couldn't let it die from exposure to the freezing weather; I had to bring it home to find out what had happened to Byeongcheol.

Hiking down a mountain with a dog on my back was a terrible idea. I was so exhausted by the time I got home that I felt ill. It was big, even though it was light; it must have been starving, as its bony ribs were visible with each breath it took. But I didn't feel any sympathy. I could kill it now and still not be satisfied when I thought of how it had snatched Seongcheol and Byeongcheol by the napes of their necks. I locked it in a crate and kept my eyes glued on the beast for the two hours it slept.

The dog let out a low growl as soon as its eyes snapped open. It lowered its body and bared its teeth, which made me hesitate. But I bent down and met its eyes. Where's your friend? I demanded. I know there's another one of you. The dog barked viciously. *Go away.*

I pushed the ball of fur I'd prepared toward the crate. I'd saved the fur collected on Seongcheol and Byeongcheol's brush. I know Seongcheol is dead, I said. But what did you do with Byeongcheol? The dog sniffed the fur and began growling again.

I picked up a syringe filled with a lethal dose of tranquilizer. Where's your friend? I yelled, and the dog barked, its eyes holding mine. *He's dead.* I held the ball of fur out again. Did Byeongcheol die, too? I tried to keep my voice steady, but it came out wobbly. The dog barked the same way again, and I threw the crate door open. Stop lying to me, I shouted, gripping the dog by the throat. I know Byeongcheol ran away. I looked everywhere and he wasn't there. That was when I felt something hard. I looked more closely and found a thin collar buried in the dog's tangled coat.

That caught me off guard, but I pretended I didn't see it. Still holding the dog by the throat, I brought the syringe close to its side. It didn't try to avoid it. It didn't try to bite or resist. I was shocked. The animal just looked at me, its throat in my hand. *I should shove the syringe in this dog, I really should,* but my hand froze when I met its eyes.

Truth be told, I had known Byeongcheol was dead. And because I knew that, I felt like I had to get my revenge like this or else go mad. But now, the dog was here before my eyes, and I couldn't kill it. I was crying, holding it by its collared throat, unable to kill or let go. Suddenly, with a rumble, the floor shuddered like an earthquake had hit. By the time I got my wits about me, I realized a vinyl-sized hole was gaping in the middle of my floor. Stunned, I let go of the dog and looked down into the hole, and there, incredibly, was Alaska.

Yu was lying like a mummy in the middle of snowy Alaska. The white cement dust had blanketed Yu's place when the ceiling caved in. What happened? I yelled down at Yu through the hole. He broke up with me, she said. Hang on, I'm coming, I said, then looked at the dog in front of me. I was so amped up that it took me some time to catch my breath. The dog lay in a corner, leaving its fate in my hands. Our eyes met. It didn't avoid my gaze; we stared at each other for a long time. I let out a long sigh. Nothing was going according to plan.

Should I go downstairs and leave the dog here? I worried about it for a bit, then decided to take it with me. The dog stayed still while I made a leash out of twine, and it obeyed when I tugged it down the emergency stairs. When Yu opened the door, she was covered in white powder. You have a dog? she asked, looking down at it. It's not mine, it's a stray, I said.

I made Yu sit on the couch and asked her what happened. She said her boyfriend caught her tailing him. All last week, she had taken sleeping pills but still couldn't sleep. Her boyfriend was taking longer to call her back, which made her more and more anxious. One day, she had gone over to his place, and when she saw him with his other girlfriend Yu had started trailing them. How did you get caught? I asked. I was driving and I accidentally hit them from behind, Yu explained. Her boyfriend dumped her on the spot, and when she got home she just stared up at the ceiling, like before. And then . . .

Yu said that she couldn't stop even though she knew she was making the hole bigger. I told her it was okay and dusted the cement powder off her head and shoulders. I wanted to talk to you, but I couldn't get hold of you, she said. I'm sorry, I was busy, I said. Looks like it, she said, looking at the stray dog. The dog was lying on its belly on the floor. Your dog stinks, she said. I told you, it's not mine, I said.

We sat on the couch together, looking up at the hole in the ceiling. I saw a very familiar table leg above. That voodoo doll, Yu started, I was thinking about it, and I think it worked. My boyfriend's girlfriend is out of my life, since he's gone, too. She coughed from all the dust. Eventually we were coughing more than we were talking, but neither of us bothered to start cleaning. As I sat next to Yu on the couch in her all-white apartment, it felt like we were stranded on a snowy mountain in Alaska. I leaned my head on her shoulder.

Should I tell her what I've been dealing with? I wondered. *Should I kick the dog out?* With another thunderous roar, more of the ceiling collapsed. The dog leaped up, startled, and paced around, and when things got quiet again it curled up in a corner. It looked like a sled dog, curled up on the snow-white floor, and the Christmas tree blanketed in cement dust looked like a small glacier. It was a quiet night, the dog, the cat, and the human each in their own heads. With all plans suspended, I watched the white dust floating in the air and thought, *Looks like it'll finally snow six meters tonight.*

Curtain Call, Extra Inning, Last Pang

If I were to impart any wisdom in my final words, I would say take your time the more rushed you are. You'll upset your stomach if you scarf down your food, you'll have forgotten something if you pack in a hurry, and you won't have a proper death if you die suddenly. I know it sounds like a joke, but it's true. I died in a freak accident last night and ended up having to roam this world.

❊

It was raining hard last night when I was on my way to the convenience store for cigarettes. I always thought the store was close to home, basically down the street in an alley, but it's a different story in a storm. The heavy downpour soaked through my clothes, and my feet kept slipping out of my flip-flops. I stopped right in front of the convenience store to shove my feet back in my flip-flops when there was a flash. I felt excruciating pain on the back of my head and then crumpled to the wet ground, unconscious.

I came to surrounded by whiteness. I stood there, baffled, until a voice greeted me from down below. Hello. I jumped a little and looked down to see a gray pigeon. You died around one fifty in the morning yesterday, said the pigeon in a grave voice. The cause of death was head injury. You were hit and killed by a falling Chinese restaurant sign, which came loose in the heavy rain and high winds. Right, that Chinese restaurant. I had decided to never set foot in it after I saw a rat gnawing on a pile of onions near the front door.

Am I a ghost? I asked. I'm sorry to inform you that you are, replied the pigeon, then went on to explain that while most people left this world instantly upon death, a final stretch of time was provided for those who died suddenly; apparently this rule was created because some ghosts in the past refused to leave for the next world, unable to accept their deaths.

The pigeon continued: Twenty-four hours from now, a button will pop up from your navel. Press it for at least three seconds and you'll vanish from this world. Once you hit a hundred hours, you'll vanish automatically, so I recommend that you press it as soon as you're ready. Go say goodbye to the people you love or do something you always dreamt of doing. The pigeon asked if I had any questions.

Am I in heaven? I asked. No, the pigeon said. How did you learn to speak human language? I asked. The pigeon said it had been working as a carrier pigeon when the development of communications technology rendered its job obsolete, but that it had made the most of its ability to convey messages and switched professions. That's when I developed the ability to converse with humans, explained the pigeon. Despite myself, I was impressed that the pigeon had succeeded in finding a new job. This bird had twice done something I'd never been able to achieve while I was alive.

The pigeon yanked me out of my thoughts. To put it simply, the bird continued, this is an after-death service provided to those who met a sudden end. If you want to know how much time you have left, you can take a look at your left wrist. I glanced at my left wrist and saw the number *100* on it. As time passes, the pigeon said, you'll turn more and more transparent, until, in the end, you vanish—*poof*.

Where do I go when I vanish? I asked. I'm sorry, the pigeon said, I don't have that information. I hesitated, then asked, I understand what you just told me, but can I just vanish now if I fully accept that I'm dead? The pigeon shook its head, telling me that I had to remain in this world for at least the next twenty-four hours; that was the rule. I let out a sigh.

Where would you like to begin your hundred hours? asked the pigeon. I told the bird I didn't have anywhere particular I wanted to be. If you're not sure, you'll go back to where you were right before death, the pigeon said. I nodded listlessly.

My surroundings gradually darkened; I looked down to discover that the pigeon was nowhere to be found. I was back in that narrow alley. The torrential rain had stopped. The pigeon had said I'd died the day before, so it must now be one fifty in the morning the following day. I looked down at my wrist at the remaining time: *99:59*. I sat on my haunches to study the spot I died in. Who found my body?

I tried to find any trace of myself under the streetlight, but nothing remained on the black asphalt road. A motorcycle drove over the spot I died in, turned the corner, and disappeared. *Well, that was fast,* I thought. Seoul forgot my death as speedily as that. Then again, the reason I liked Seoul was because it was so crowded you could disappear. No single individual stood out.

❊

That was how I found myself a ghost, roaming this world. I used to think my cigarette habit would kill me, but never like this. You never knew what could happen in life, and that was the same in death apparently. I was given a very weird extension. You could say it was like the curtain call after a performance, the extra inning at a baseball game, the last pang in the *Anipang* game.

I wasn't planning to use all one hundred hours. When that button popped up in twenty-four hours I would instantly press it. The problem was that I had no idea how to spend this day. Should I go home? But then I remembered that my place was basically a garbage dump. I wondered if I should wait till morning and hit the owner of that Chinese restaurant over the head, but decided it wasn't worth it.

I wandered down dark, empty streets, wondering where a good place to die would be. Well, no, I was already dead—

where would be the best place to vanish? The first candidate was a suite in a five-star hotel. But even if the five-star hotel was incredible, I was sick and tired of being stuck inside all day. The second candidate was by the ocean. It might be nice to lie on a quiet beach and vanish, but it was summer, peak vacation season, and it would be too crowded. My last idea was the 63 Building. The 63 Building always popped into my head whenever I tried to think of a nice place. That large gold bar–like building had been the pride of the entire nation until taller structures began popping up all over. We had a lot in common now—it was just as unexciting and lame as me. I decided I didn't want to go to the 63 Building.

At one point I had been proud of myself. I'd survived by taking all manner of part-time jobs, and I managed to graduate college even though it took me a long time. But my world had grown smaller over the last two years as I kept failing to land a real job. In that narrower space I had no room for lovers or friends. I let them all go without a proper goodbye. Also gone: a stable living situation and balanced meals. As time passed, even the stuff that disappeared became increasingly insignificant: the volume of my hair, the regularity of my periods, the movies I watched every weekend morning, the baseball team I cheered for.

In the end, even job applications fell away. At some point I'd started writing a will instead of filling out job applications. I'd been working on my will the night I died, looking out my tiny window, watching the rain come down, listening to my neighbors making a ruckus. If someone were to open up my laptop, they would discover my will running hundreds of pages long, saved in my job application folder.

I took a long walk until I got to the neighborhood café where I used to be a regular. This wasn't the place I wanted to vanish from, but it was the only place I could think of. The doors were locked, so I settled in a chair on the patio. I could see a huge glowing electronic billboard in between the thicket of buildings across the way. Ads were cycling through, even in the middle of the night. An ad for soda, an ad for a designer bag, an ad for an upcoming movie—things that had become irrelevant to me flashed by. The movie, featuring a mutant creature, would open in a week; by that time, I wouldn't be here. It was starting to sink in that I was dead.

This must be why they had a rule requiring you to spend at least a day in this world, I thought. For some reason I felt lonely now. I leaned back in my chair. Was my funeral being held right now? Would my family have heard the news? I hadn't been in touch for so long; nobody would have their number.

Leaving such complicated tasks to the living, I sat waiting for the sun to rise, and I almost fainted from shock when it finally did. My body appeared clear under the bright sunlight. Death seemed to have leached all the color from me. The prominent veins against my skin, the fingerprints that had once been engraved on the pads of my fingers—neither were visible. I really must be dead, I murmured to myself.

The café owner arrived not long after. I followed him in and watched him wipe down the tables and make coffee. He was a kind person who would sit behind the counter and read quietly when business was slow. It made me sad that I couldn't drink his coffee anymore.

Still, it was nice to be back at the café, and since I wasn't visible I could people watch freely. I listened to conversations as if listening to the radio. I observed things I hadn't been able to see before. Even though I was dead, people still were falling in love, still hated others, and, from time to time, still wanted to die. How in the world did these urges continue without waning? I felt so overwhelmed that I wanted to die, even though I was already dead.

In the afternoon two girls who'd failed in their quest to buy Coldplay tickets sat next to me. The concert was that evening. We'll get another chance, right? asked the girl with the bob. No, said the girl with the long hair. But we'll be able to see them at some point in our lives, right? the first girl asked. No, the girl with the long hair told her. Should we try to buy tickets off a scalper? asked the girl with the bob. But they're going for a million won, the second girl replied. At that, the girl with the bob buried her head in her arms in despair and went on and on about why they'd failed to nab the tickets, what they could have done if they'd been successful, and what they should have done to buy them.

Music never interested me much and I'd never been to a concert, but their discussion about failure and success, about how it was their only chance, kept needling me. Would I feel like I'd achieved something if I went to such a huge venue? I was bored sitting in the café anyway, so I got up.

❁

I had to take the subway to the venue. I thought I'd be able to fly or go through walls as a ghost, but none of that cool stuff was possible. I did get to sit in a priority seat, though, and most of my fellow passengers got off at Sports Complex station.

I was headed to the exit, jostled by the crowd, when I heard a woman shouting for help. The voice got louder and louder as I went down the passageway, but nobody around me reacted. Could no one hear the cry for help? I looked around and discovered that the calls were coming from inside a storeroom at the end of the passageway. I peeked in the open doorway and saw only cleaning supplies and a large vacuum cleaner. It had a piece of paper stuck to it that said *Out of Order*. Nobody was there. I was about to leave when I heard the voice call out, Who's there? Can you hear me?

I looked back. A talking vacuum? I found myself saying. I'm not a talking vacuum, I'm trapped inside, came a reply. Taken aback, I asked if she was a ghost, and she said she was. How did you end up in there? I asked. She said she had bumped into a custodian as she walked through the station last night. She was about to go around, but the custodian had pushed the vacuum toward her, catching her in the strong suction of the machine. The machine stopped working the instant it sucked up the ghost.

I tried to get the ghost out, but the enormous round compartment wouldn't open. I tugged and pulled until I collapsed next to it. I can't open it, I said. No, it doesn't seem like you can, the vacuum said. Are you in pain? I asked. No, she said, explaining that she just couldn't stand to be mixed up with dust and random bits of trash and gum wrappers and tangles of hair.

Last night another ghost came by but said there wasn't enough time and left, she said. I guess a hundred hours isn't enough time to spend it on someone else, I said. That's true, the vacuum said, then asked if I was on my way to the concert. How did you know? I asked. Otherwise why would there be so many ghosts here? she asked. Feeling deflated, I said, I guess everyone has the same basic idea even in death.

The vacuum told me there was something more important for her than just seeing Coldplay. I wanted to stand onstage, she confessed. I was in training for seven years to be part of a K-pop group, but I died before my debut.

That made me want to get her out of that vacuum no matter what. She still had a dream, and she was wasting her time. I got up and tried to open the compartment again, but couldn't.

That's okay, the vacuum said, go to the concert. What are you going to do? I asked. I can always vanish, the vacuum said matter-of-factly. I thought it over. I didn't mind not seeing the concert, but I also didn't want to spend my remaining time here in the storeroom. I'll be back after the concert, I promised the vacuum. Go stand onstage for me, she said. I told her I'd try. I checked my wrist: I had eighty-five hours remaining, nine more hours before my twenty-four hours were up.

•

The stadium was crowded. I skipped the long lines and went straight to the second level. I leaned on the railing to watch people. It didn't really feel like I'd accomplished anything. Watching the enormous stadium fill with people actually made it feel less real. Where did all these people come from? A countdown started on the huge screen onstage.

When it hit *0*, the stage lights flashed and Coldplay came out. With a roar, the audience waved their light sticks, which rippled like water, and paper confetti fell from the ceiling. I stood subdued in the excited crowd, under the snowfall of confetti. The concert started, but nothing lit up inside me. I wasn't elated or excited; in fact, I didn't feel any emotion. Even as I watched the stage, it felt like I was observing something happening far, far away.

Watching the stage and the crowd bathed in colorful light, I realized something. Slowly, I raised my arm in front of me. A beam of red light disappeared the moment it touched my arm. It was the same with other colored lights. No matter which light touched me, my arm stayed an unchanging black. I looked at my dark arm, then at the stage and the audience glowing under multicolored lights. I left the arena before the end of the first song.

In the subway station, I planned to get back to the vacuum, but this time the storeroom door was closed. I had to wait on a bench for over an hour until a custodian arrived with keys. It was dark in the storeroom, and I couldn't see very well, but there I finally felt at peace.

When the custodian left, I rapped on the vacuum. Who is it? the vacuum said, sounding surprised. It's me, I said, I told you I'd be back. I thought you were just saying that, she said. Is it already over? Yeah, I lied. How was it? she asked. It was fine, I told her. It was loud and over-the-top. The vacuum noticed I was being vague and said, You didn't go to the concert, did you? I said I did, but soon confessed that I left in the middle of the first song.

Why'd you do that for? she asked. It just felt weird, I told her. You shouldn't have thought about anything else while you were there, she admonished. Without answering, I stared at the dust floating in the air. The vacuum was right. I shouldn't have thought about anything at all while I was at the concert. I was terrified by the fact that the people all around me were alive, vibrantly alive; it was the first time I was scared about being dead. If the button had popped up I would have pressed it right then and there. A brief silence hung between us. You should leave the next time the door opens, the vacuum said. I don't have that much time left anyway. I told her I would.

This strange night deepened as we sat in the small storeroom. My feelings careened up and down constantly, like they were on a roller coaster. I felt relieved then lonely, nervous then reassured. *I shouldn't think about anything right now, either,* I thought. I leaned against the vacuum. A little later, the vacuum said, Thank you for coming back.

❋

The CEO of her management company told her she could make her debut only if she lost fifteen kilos, so she tried to lose the weight any way she could. That was how she died. She went back to the studio in her ghost form; she clamped a hand over the singing mouth of a trainee and gripped on to the ankles of another who was dancing. She punched the CEO in the face. None of them blinked an eye, but she'd spent two whole days doing her best to antagonize them. That wasn't my plan in the beginning, she told me, but they were redoing the choreography even before my funeral was over, changing it from a five-person to a four-person formation. I told her she did good.

What did you do when you were alive? she asked me. I told her I'd been an office worker. I didn't know why I said that. When she asked me how I'd died, I told her I'd died from overwork. You shouldn't have worked so hard to only benefit others, she chided. Tell me about it, I said.

Don't you feel trapped being stuck inside that thing for two whole days? I asked, changing the subject. It's okay, the vacuum said, I have an active imagination. What have you been imagining? I asked. I imagine that I'm onstage, she said. My management company gave me image training. She explained how she'd hold the mic, what it would feel like to be onstage, even every bead of sweat coasting down her face, in the most minute detail. She said she'd been imagining this for such a long time that all she had to do was close her eyes to stand onstage. It was useful now, stuck as she was in the vacuum.

Why are you still here, anyway? I finally asked, unable to help myself. It's all over now. That was something I'd been wanting to ask her from the beginning. I wanted to know why she was working so hard when she was just going to vanish in the end. What did she think she would gain by sticking it out like this?

She didn't answer for a while, then said she couldn't bring herself to push the button. I worked so hard to be a singer, she said, and it will have been for nothing if I press the button.

I didn't have anything to say to that. What was it like to live life like that? Living like you had something to protect until the bitter end. She said she understood if I thought she was pathetic. No, I actually envy you, I said, and she replied that she envied me. What's to envy? I asked. If you were an office worker you would have gotten a regular salary, she said. I never made any money my whole life, not ever. I laughed at that. What's so funny? she asked, and I told her I was laughing because I found myself pathetic. As I laughed, my stomach itched, and when I reached down I felt a round, hard button. I suddenly hushed, and she asked what was wrong. Nothing, I said. I wasn't planning to tell her that my button popped up. It didn't seem like a terrible idea to stay a few more hours.

That quiet night, after the last train left the station, the vacuum began singing. *Mm mm, mm mm mm.* What's that song? I asked. It would have been my first single if I'd managed to make my debut, she said. It doesn't have any lyrics? I asked. Not yet, she said. I was going to tell her, *You should write the lyrics yourself*, but stopped myself. This right here was nice.

Mm mm, mm mm mm, I hummed along in my head, when a fuzzy human shape reared up before my eyes. Who are you?! I shouted. It was too dark for me to tell if it was a man or a woman. Did someone come in? asked the vacuum in alarm. I didn't hear the door open. An older man's voice came from the fuzzy shape: I couldn't be sure, so I came to see for myself, but you really are ghosts. Don't worry, he continued. I'm a ghost like the two of you. I died a few days ago.

How did you get in when the door's closed? I asked suspiciously. As time passed my body got fuzzier and light as air, the man said, and after ninety-nine hours I was able to pass through doors and walls. Then can you get into this vacuum cleaner? I asked. She's trapped inside. The man said he'd try and approached the machine.

What's going on? shouted the vacuum. Just hold my hand and come out, the man instructed, and reached toward the vacuum. It was true that he could pass through walls, as his hand disappeared inside the vacuum. He began tugging. I grabbed him around the waist and pulled. After some tugging we could feel the ghost being slowly dragged out. I didn't know how much time passed, but eventually an amorphous, dough-like thing was pulled out of the long hose, through the head. Depleted, the man and I sank to the floor and waited for the lump to take human shape.

Soon I was facing a thin young woman. Thank you, she said, brushing herself off. I really didn't want to die buried in trash.

How did you know we were here? I asked the man. I didn't think it was living people singing in a subway storeroom at four in the morning, he said. It turned out he had been a station employee when he was alive. He explained that he'd come to see the first train pull into the station when he heard us singing.

We had to leave the storeroom, if only to watch the first train pull in. The issue was that it was impossible for the two of us to pass through the metal door. The girl checked her wrist and announced that she had three and a half hours left. I finally managed to get out of that vacuum, and now I'm trapped in the storeroom, she said. The overnight cleanup crew will be done soon, the man said. Then we can all go out together.

What if you miss the first train? I asked, and he answered that he wanted to fulfill his duties as a station employee. You two are customers, he said. Do you consider freeloaders to be customers, too? I asked. Of course, he said. In the end we decided to sit on the floor, all three of us, until someone opened the door. What was that song you were singing earlier? asked the station employee. I've never heard it before. I was about to tell him, but the girl said, Oh, I just made it up.

Ten minutes later, two custodians entered the storeroom. We slipped out while they were organizing their carts. Luckily the first train hadn't arrived yet. Would you like company? the girl asked. The man hesitated briefly, then said he would appreciate it. The girl asked if I wanted to join them, and I said I would.

We sat side by side on a bench on the platform servicing line 2. Thank you, said the station employee, who was sitting between us, his shoulders hunched nervously forward. To be honest I was scared to be alone. Why did you want to see the first train pull in? asked the girl. Because I need courage, he said. He explained that when he was alive, he would watch the first train arrive whenever he felt distraught. That when he saw the first train pull up to the quiet platform, like a promise, like magic, sometimes like a miracle, the courage he didn't have would bubble up.

Do you think it hurts when we vanish? asked the station employee, staring straight ahead. I'm sure it won't, I said. He nodded slowly. We heard the announcement that the train was entering the station, accompanied by the familiar jingle. It pulled in, its headlights bright, and just as the dozens of doors flung open, the man turned into a small spark and vanished. The spark died out and let out a small sound—*poof*.

The pigeon had described what would happen accurately, I realized. We sat there for a while in silence even after he vanished. *This must be the end, that's all there was to it, and there's nothing waiting for us,* I thought, and at the same time I had the silly thought that the spark had been beautiful.

What's your name? I asked, breaking the silence, and she snorted: Now you're asking? A beat later, she said it was Irang. That's a pretty name, I said. Because it's not my real name, she said, it's the stage name I was going to use on my debut. I told Irang that she should do what she wanted to do, now that she had escaped the storeroom. But she shook her head. What's the point? she asked as she looked down at herself. She didn't have much time left; she was becoming fainter, just like the station employee. I knew why she was saying that, but still . . .

I was starting to feel antsy. Here was someone who wanted to stand onstage even after death. She threw punches at people who'd hurt her. She couldn't lose that verve now. I knew better than most that losing that spark was sometimes worse than actually dying. As I thought about this, another train pulled up. I had an idea as I watched people get on and off. I whispered into her ear, even though nobody could hear me. She burst out laughing. She liked it.

We took the next train four stops to Gangnam station. When we emerged from the subway the sun was so bright that it could make you dizzy, but I felt good. Even at this early hour people were out and about. Laughing, Irang and I passed by tired pedestrians. Everything was funny: the too-clear sky, the pigeons pretending to be clueless birds, the buildings as gray as our bodies.

She grabbed my hand as we crossed the street. Her warm hand felt fragile, like it would disintegrate if I held on too tight. Nothing was scary when I was holding her hand, so I confessed to her: I'm not actually an office worker, and I didn't die from overwork. I was going to the convenience store for cigarettes, and a sign fell and hit me on the head and that's how I died.

Irang smiled and told me it was better that I died that way. Did it hurt a lot when you were dying? she asked, and I shrugged: I don't really remember.

She was becoming brighter and lighter as we walked. Like air, like wind. Eventually she was floating, even as she held my hand. More and more people poured into the streets the closer we neared the morning rush, and we started running to avoid them. We never got out of breath no matter how far we ran, and I looked at the streets as we ran through them. Goodbye, you infernal Seoul. Goodbye, loud signs. Goodbye, plastic cups discarded on the bus stop bench. Goodbye everything, goodbye, goodbye.

We went up to the roof of a building. This is the perfect place, right? Irang asked, and I told her it was. We faced each other, our features blurry. I'm off, then, said Irang. See you later, I said, and told her I wasn't just saying that. She smiled and nodded. And that was it. She walked down the stairs, and I stood by myself on the roof, looking out at the city. It was 6:51 in the morning.

❊

That day, at 7:13 a.m., a huge electronic billboard located along Gangnam-daero experienced an error lasting three minutes and twenty-one seconds.

Drivers caught in traffic, pedestrians waiting for the green light at the crosswalk, people looking out the window—they all witnessed the electronic display, which had been playing an ad for a designer suit, suddenly turn black. A small white circle appeared in the dead center of the black screen. Everyone watched as the circle grew bigger. *She did it,* I thought. I'd whispered in her ear on the subway platform that she should go onstage for her debut performance, and she did it.

Three minutes and twenty-one seconds.

The length of a song playing in its entirety.

For those three minutes and twenty-one seconds, I watched Irang in her amazing debut performance without blinking. She had waited forever for this moment. I imagined a soul leaping boldly into the screen. The white circle grew bigger and the screen turned brighter, and finally, when the screen turned completely white, something incredible happened. The screen began to illuminate the city. That white light, bright as snow, made all the darkened rooms, all the dark alleys of the city, glow brilliantly. Watching people standing in that flood of light, I clapped as hard as I could. Then I had an odd feeling. I would miss all this. The many faces, movies on weekend mornings, a baseball drawing an arc in the air—I thought I could love them again. I closed my eyes to imagine them one last time.

Author's Note

As I was putting the final touches on my first story collection, I read about Gobliatron, hero of an arctic country. Gobliatron was frozen solid on a field of ice from a single glance by a machine man. Stuck in place, he started to think hot. He thought hot until he began running a fever, and when his fever spiked, the ice melted, and our hero became free.

I came across this story in Siri Hustvedt's *The Blazing World* and liked it so much that I wrote it down in a notebook and kept paging it open to reread it. I loved that what saved Gobliatron was Gobliatron himself, that thinking hot accomplished something incredible. I've always had too many thoughts and at one point considered it a flaw that needed fixing. But as I wrote *With the Heart of the Ghost*, I realized that thinking could lead to freedom. The more I think, the freer I can be. I can do this at any time.

I'd like to note that the eight stories in this collection were born from the following vignettes:

- a mirror by the foot of a bed;
- the highway I could see from my room in the middle of the night;

- dying plants inside a shuttered shop;
- water flowing;
- water gushing;
- light reaching the screen of an independent movie theater located in the basement of a building and light reaching trees planted along the street;
- Tree, the name of a tree;
- the first train of the day and a taxi at midnight;
- neuroses and phantoms;
- day-like nights and the many night-like days.

If my stories hold any amount of brightness and warmth, they come from what I owe to the people I love.

To my mom, the person I respect most in the world: you taught me to believe and be brave.

To my grandfather, who handed down the love I have for people; to my brother, Sungmin, who knows me better than I know myself; to Youjung, who reads each of my stories and leaves me long messages late at night—thank you.

To my Korean editor, Gihyun Jeong—I cherished every step of making this book with you.

Finally, I am deeply grateful to my Korean publisher, Minumsa, for unreservedly cheering on a rookie writer.

I promise to keep working hard.

Lim Sunwoo
Spring 2022